The door was flun[...] elderly laughing w[...] [...]ed, "Surprise!"

One of them held a bough of something over his head, then stood on her tiptoes and kissed him soundly on the cheek.

"Marlys, do you have mistletoe?" he teased.

She blushed and nodded. "Yes, I do."

"Can I borrow it?" he asked with a wink.

Abbey's stomach twisted with anticipation and anxiety. Surely he wouldn't…surely he would.

Which did she want?

"Sweet's going to smooch his sugarplum," someone in the group crowed.

"That's right," he said, his eyes twinkling as he turned to look at Abbey.

Her heart and her mind waged war. She wanted him to take advantage of the mistletoe, and yet she didn't. For a moment, time held its breath.

Then he announced, his warm brown eyes twinkling, "The first kiss goes to my favorite girl."

All heads swiveled with one accord to look at Abbey. She knew she was blushing, but there wasn't a thing she could do but stand stock-still and wait for her fate.

Mike raised the mistletoe and…

JANET SPAETH

figures she has it all, living between the prairies of North Dakota and the north woods of Minnesota. She has been blessed with the "world's best family." From tallest to shortest, they are husband Kevin, daughter Megan, son Nick and cat Quicksilver. Janet is honored to write stories that reflect the happiness of love guided by God.

JANET SPAETH

Candy Cane Calaboose

HEARTSONG
PRESENTS

To M.E. Froelich
Friends 4Ever

"This is the day which the Lord hath made;
we will rejoice and be glad in it."
—*Psalms* 118:24

LOVE INSPIRED BOOKS

PLEASE RECYCLE
THIS PRODUCT IS RECYCLABLE

Recycling programs
for this product may
not exist in your area.

ISBN-13: 978-0-373-48761-5

CANDY CANE CALABOOSE

Heartsong Presents/February 2014

First published by Barbour Publishing, Inc.

Copyright © 2001 by Janet Spaeth

All Scripture quotations are taken from the King James Version of the Bible.

Cover illustration by Kay Salem

www.Harlequin.com

Printed in U.S.A.

Chapter 1

"No, no, stop!" Abbey Jensen yelled futilely at the package that slithered off the towering pile of decorated Christmas socks. But the package continued on its wayward course, sliding through the slots of the grating that blocked the front entrance of Trends and landing on the highly polished floor of the empty mall just outside the store.

She looked around her as if a solution beyond the only obvious one would suddenly appear. But nothing materialized.

She was going to have to open the security gate and retrieve the package from the mall floor.

She just wanted to go home. She'd been at the store since shortly after seven that morning, and it was now—she glanced at her watch and nearly gasped—almost eleven at night. At this rate, she might as well just go ahead and set up a cot in the store—if she could find a spot that wasn't covered with racks or shelves. Her store was getting crowded with the holiday displays that arrived daily.

Abbey turned her key in the grid work's lock and winced as it groaned open. The sound echoed through the empty mall. The gate raised itself no more than a yard above the floor and stuck.

It wasn't the first time. She ducked under the gate and snatched up the socks from the gleaming tile of the outer mall. Glaring at the recalcitrant grid work, she kicked the bars angrily. "Piece of junk—"

As if in reply, the gate slammed shut.

Her keys were still dangling in the lock on the other side of the gate, tantalizingly just out of reach. Abbey tried to reach the keys, but her hand wouldn't fit through the grating. She was stuck inside the cavernous Cedar Mall.

What should she do? The mall doors were set up so that she could leave through any of them without setting off an alarm, but then what? The keys to her car and her house were on the same ring as the store's keys—on the other side of the grating.

Frustration rose in her like an angry fountain. She could see the keys, but they might as well be in Timbuktu.

She set off through the mall in search of a security guard.

That meant she had to run the gauntlet that the mall management had placed in her way. Cedar Mall looked more like it was situated at the North Pole than in Northern Mills, Minnesota. The numerous Christmas decorations, normally so festive, now looked merely stupid. At Santa's workshop, an elf held a little silver hammer that was minus its tip. Santa himself, lit only from the faint glow of security lights, appeared old and tired. Only the plastic reindeer seemed to have any personality. One of them faced her as if ready to take a bite out of her.

The expression on the reindeer's face reminded her that she was hungry. If she didn't get something to eat pretty soon, she'd take a bite out of the reindeer. She hurried past the display.

It was just one of many ahead of her. The mall owners had decided that this year they would go all out. Games and kiosks, exhibitions and artwork, all jostled each other for room. She ignored them and headed toward the mall office. Security was usually there at night.

It wasn't that she had anything against Christmas. Christmas was, in fact, one of her favorite holidays. At least it had been when she was a little girl. Now that her family was scattered across the continent, she had to spend Christmas alone. As a store manager, she no longer had the luxury of leaving Minnesota to spend the holidays with her parents in their home in Connecticut.

And the specter of spending Christmas alone was enough to put a damper on even the most fervid Yule fan. The solution was easy: She didn't think about it.

What she needed to think about now was getting in touch with mall security.

A light in another store a bit further down gave her an idea. Tuck's Toys, Mike's store…she breathed a sigh of relief.

She and Mike Tucker had been friends since they were children. Not good friends, and certainly not as close as their parents would have liked, but friends nevertheless. He'd let her in to use his phone.

As she peered through the grating of Tuck's Toys, she saw a head moving behind a display and she called out, "Excuse me? Is someone there? Mike?"

A familiar face popped up. "Abbey!"

Abbey breathed a sigh of relief. Never before had Mike's round brown eyes and dark blond hair seemed so welcoming.

"I'm locked out of the store, Mike," she said. "Can I use your phone to call Security?"

"No problem." He turned the key in the grid work of his store.

His gate, she noticed, didn't groan and screech the way hers did. And it didn't catch part way up. She was going to have to talk to the mall management about hers.

She ducked in under the opening grid and followed him to the phone as he asked, "Are you working late tonight too?"

Abbey nodded. "I wanted to rearrange the entrance displays. What about you?"

"Oh, I took a break earlier. I ran out to Golden Meadows to see Grandma, and I had dinner with her out there."

Her stomach growled in response to the word *dinner*. "How's she doing?" Abbey had never met his grandmother, but she knew that Mike was devoted to her.

"Pretty good. She's a cool lady. You should come

with me someday and meet her. I think you'd like her."

Not a chance, Abbey thought. Maybe Mike liked going to Golden Meadows—after all, his grandmother lived there—but for her it would just be a visit to a place where old people went to die. No, thank you.

"And then," Mike continued, as if he hadn't noticed her chill, "it was back to work." He motioned toward an open box. "More Wag-A-Muffins."

"Wag-A-Muffins?" She stopped and stared at him.

"Have you been living on another planet, or what?" He grinned and reached into the box. "This is a Wag-A-Muffin, the hottest toy in the universe. By noon tomorrow, we'll be sold out."

He held up a small brown stuffed dog. "Watch this." He stroked the toy animal's back, and the tail curled. "Neat, huh? There are about thirty-five different animals, although I doubt that I have all of them here."

She touched it, and the tail lifted into a curlicue. "It's really cute."

Silence met her statement, and she raised her eyes to see him leaning against a display of computer games, a contemplative soft smile on his face.

"What's the matter?" she said and immediately regretted the belligerent tone.

He shook his head and smiled brightly at her. "Nothing. It's just that for a moment I thought I saw a streak of humanity in you."

She glared at him. The old familiar taunt he'd leveled at her since they were children still hurt, although she'd never let him know it.

"The only warmth that flows through my bloodstream comes in at a steady 98.6, thank you very much," she shot back.

"What about when you get a fever? Oh, I know," he interrupted himself as she tried to speak. "You don't get sick. That's for wimps."

"I don't have time for it." Abbey shrugged off the argument. "Actually, I don't have time for anything right now except to head back to my store and get my keys. I want to go home. I'm hungry, and I'm tired. It's been a long day."

"And they're not going to get any shorter now that the Christmas season is gaining on us," he agreed amiably.

He handed her the phone, and within minutes the two of them were walking back toward Trends.

"What do you think of this Christmas Village idea?" Mike asked as they walked by Center Court, where an entire town was set up. Each tiny building was in fact a kiosk with a seasonal specialty. Stuff Your Stockings sold leg wear of all kinds, Lollipop Time sold candy, and Piñata Pete's sold piḼatas in imaginative shapes.

"It's, well, a bit much." Abbey wrinkled her nose at the display. "I can understand why they're doing it, and it's already bringing in lots of foot traffic just to see it, but it's too busy for me."

"You know, it's not all that the mall management has planned," he said, but Abbey had lost interest.

She spied the security guard ahead and sprinted toward the gate.

She was dimly aware of the fact that Mike had

dropped back, but all she could think of was what awaited her: a hot dinner, a warm bath, and a cozy bed.

Mike watched her head for the guard as if the man held the keys to heaven itself.

Mike knew he was frowning, but he couldn't help himself. He'd always cared for Abbey, but her aloofness had kept him at a distance.

Still, she had a talent for fashion. With her sleek black hair, clear gray eyes, and willowy figure, she could be a fashion model. She also had an instinctive feel for business that he envied. When he'd heard that she was taking over Trends, he was delighted. The fashionable store had suffered under poor management and was near closing, but she had brought it back to life.

But she'd accomplished it at great expense. He'd seen the lines of exhaustion etched around her eyes. He wanted to take her in his arms and hold her, let her rest her head against his shoulder, while he breathed in the fresh scent of her perfume.

But that would never happen. She'd made that clear. No relationships, no ties. She was building her résumé, she'd told him, and she had no time for anything that would swerve her off that course.

He watched as she stumbled slightly. She was fatigued beyond even her capability. She was definitely too tired to drive, but he knew she'd never admit it, and she'd certainly never accept a ride from him. Abbey would insist on driving herself home.

Mike shut his eyes and offered a quick prayer.

Father, take care of her. See her home safely. She is so worn out.

His gaze stayed on her as the guard opened the gate and she reentered the store. It took him less than a second to know what to do. As quickly as he could, he hurried back to his store, switched off the lights, and closed the gate. Then he retraced his steps, looping around Christmas Village, and left through the door of the mall that was closest to Trends.

His breath froze in his nostrils as he stood outside, scanning the expanse before him. The parking lot was empty. Or almost empty.

His instincts had been right. He could see her car pulling out of one of the far-off slots where mall employees were supposed to park, and from the pause before she switched gears, he could tell how deep her exhaustion was.

He followed her home, staying a discreet distance behind, and left only as he saw her put the key in the door of her house. She would be safe. He smiled and let out a sigh of relief.

Abbey leaned against the storm door, letting the cool metal refresh her tired forehead. Tomorrow she'd have to find some time to shovel the steps. The snow was so drifted, even this early in the season, that the door wouldn't fully open.

But the snow was more compacted than she'd figured. She dug into the drift with her toe to clear it.

It wasn't all snow. There was something there.

She reached down and burrowed through the snow until her fingers closed around a squarish form. It was a package, she realized, as she dusted the snow off.

And, from the emerald green writing on the address, she knew immediately whom it was from.

Aunt Luellen. Loopy Aunt Luellen.

She opened the door and dropped the package inside the entryway as she shrugged out of her coat. She was so tired. But first she'd have to take care of this soggy package on her floor. It was already dripping into a rapidly spreading puddle.

Microwavable meatloaf was just moments away. Flannel pajamas were waiting for her. A nice comfortable bed was around the corner. A quick face wash— she was just too exhausted for a bath—a few moments to brush her teeth, and she'd be asleep.

It was a lovely thought.

But Aunt Luellen was, well, Aunt Luellen.

And the package was wet. Whatever was in it needed to be rescued. She sighed and opened the sodden package.

She blinked once. Twice. Three times. But the image remained.

Yellow fuzzy slippers with a grinning frog on the toe of each—that's what Aunt Luellen had given her. And the eyes on the frogs were bright blue plastic gems. Aunt Luellen was even loopier than ever.

A note fell from the toe of one of the slippers and Abbey unfolded it. Maybe this would give her a clue as to why on earth her aunt thought that this was an appropriate gift for a woman who owned only one pair of jeans, for whom comfortable shoes were two-inch heels.

"Claire: Every time that you wear these slippers, look at the toes and tell yourself that this day is a jewel, perfect, and ideal. If life at Golden Meadows is getting you down, look at where the jewels are—and smile! Wishing you great hoppy-ness always, today, and many tomorrows, Luellen."

Claire? Her name wasn't Claire. Aunt Luellen had gone from loopy to lunatic. Suddenly, through the fog of exhaustion, she realized what was going on. The slippers weren't meant for her. She had no idea who "Claire" was, although she was obviously one of Aunt Luellen's cronies if she lived at Golden Meadows.

Abbey sighed. She'd have to get the slippers to whoever this Claire woman was. But she didn't have the time to do that—she hadn't even had time to eat dinner. How could she fit in a trip to a retirement home? Besides, she told herself grumpily, she did not want to go to Golden Meadows. If her head weren't so clogged with a desperate need for sleep, she'd be able to figure it out.

She laid the slippers aside, planning to deal with them in the morning, and another bit of paper fell out of the other toe. "This is the day which the Lord hath made; we will rejoice and be glad in it."

The Bible. That sounded like Aunt Luellen. The woman had the whole book memorized, or so it had always seemed to Abbey. Aunt Luellen could quote Scripture with an astonishing ease. Of course, she was a missionary, so she lived and breathed religion, but nevertheless, her ability was uncanny.

Religion. That was where Abbey and Aunt Luellen parted ways. Sometime, when Abbey was established in her career and had gotten her MBA, she'd look into it again. Clearly, religion took a lot of time, and that was one thing she didn't have.

Time—and sleep. "And food," she said to the

frogs, whose bright blue eyes sparkled back at her. Meatloaf would take too long. She reached into a box of sugar cookies and held one out toward the slippers. "Froggy want a cookie?"

Abbey shook her head. Any longer with the slippers and she'd be as loopy as Aunt Luellen.

But a moment of clarity came right before sleep claimed her.

Mike.

His grandmother lived at Golden Meadows. He went there all the time. She'd give the slippers to him tomorrow, and he could take them out there to their rightful owner—whoever "Claire" was—and she'd be finished with the whole messy thing.

Abbey smiled happily. Mike would take care of everything. She just knew it.

Chapter 2

"No."

"What do you mean, 'No'?" Abbey asked as they stood outside Tuck's Toys where she'd come to visit Mike.

"Simply that. No. I won't take the present for you."

"But why not?" She could not believe what she was hearing. Why wouldn't he do this one little favor for her? "You're going out there anyway, right?"

He nodded.

"Then why not take it with you?"

"Nope."

His refusal had her flabbergasted. It didn't make any sense at all.

"You should take it out to her. For one thing," he said, "this Claire probably has your present. And besides, it just would be the Christian thing to do for your aunt Luellen."

Abbey barely restrained herself from snorting. Christian, indeed. Just because Aunt Luellen had turned her life over to the church didn't mean that she, Abbey Jensen, should act all holy. Religion wasn't one of those things that ran in the family, like red hair or big ear lobes.

"I'm going out there tonight, and I can give you a ride if you like," he offered.

"You're going out there? Just take the stupid slippers with you and be done with it, then. I can't understand why you won't." She knew she sounded like a petulant child, but she couldn't help herself. "It's no big deal."

"And I can't understand why you won't go," he parried. "'It's no big deal.'"

His words, slung back at her like that, sounded terrible.

But the fact was, she did not want to go to Golden Meadows. The thought of being surrounded, even for a minute or two, by old people was awful. That's why she liked the mall; it was young and very much alive.

"I'm going at five-thirty," Mike continued, as if he hadn't noticed anything wrong.

Abbey breathed a sigh of relief. She absolutely couldn't go. "I'm the only one in the store then."

Mike shrugged. "You deal with this on your own schedule. I go at five-thirty so I can have dinner with my grandmother. It means a lot to her."

He turned to leave, but he paused and faced her again. "It really wouldn't take you long. For about fifteen minutes of your time—which I know is pre-cious—you could make two women very happy."

Abbey could feel herself frowning. "Two women? Oh, you mean Aunt Luellen and this Claire woman."

He smiled at her. "That's right. I know that most of the people at Golden Meadows love visitors, but even if Claire is a total recluse who hates everybody and doesn't want to see anyone for the rest of her natural days, you do have her Christmas present from your aunt. Give it to her. Not only is it hers and not yours, but Abbey, it's Christmas!"

He was making this difficult, she thought as he walked away. What he didn't know about her, what he couldn't know about her, was that her heart was made of marshmallow fluff. She just had it cased inside steel.

She'd work on it. She'd figure out some way to get the slippers to Claire.

Abbey walked back to Trends, scowling at the mechanized group of carolers that sang outside the music store. Noise. Just what this world needed. More noise.

Once, just once, she was going to say it, and she did so at the Dickens village: "Bah, humbug."

Christmas didn't have to be all this complicated. And it certainly didn't have to be this loud!

The evening shift crew arrived on time, and Abbey found herself with an hour and a half free. She had wandered back to the evening dresses and began un-necessarily straightening the already neat rack, when she heard two teenaged girls giggling together.

"Look at these! Aren't these a hoot?"

One of the girls, Abbey saw, was showing the other one something in a bag.

Then, to Abbey's astonishment, the girl pulled out a pair of yellow fuzzy slippers, complete with frog faces on the toes.

"Those are like the coolest slippers ever!" the other girl gushed. "Where did you get them? I don't care if I am supposed to be shopping for my mutant brother, I've got to get some for myself!"

The two girls briefly examined a display of jewelry before ambling out of the store.

Abbey didn't believe in signs, not really, but she had to admit it: This was clearly a sign.

"Okay, that does it!" she said to the heavily beaded green gown she was holding.

"Excuse me?" A woman browsing through the evening jackets on the other side of the aisle looked at her curiously and pulled her purse a bit closer to her side.

Abbey tried to disguise her embarrassment with a laugh. "Sorry! Talking to myself!"

The woman smiled. "I understand. I've got five kids and sometimes I talk to myself just to have an adult conversation. Honey, whatever it is that you've just decided to do, you go for it!"

Abbey laughed, but she watched thoughtfully as the woman moved on. Go for it. That's exactly what she was going to do.

Mike smiled as the elderly woman next to him tugged on his sleeve. "Mike, dear, could you please play 'Red Sails in the Sunset'?"

"Sure, Grandma."

He was sharing a piano bench with her. His grandmother had lost her ability to walk, and her sight wasn't very good any longer, but her hearing was as sharp as ever.

She loved music, and soon after she had moved into Golden Meadows, she had enlisted him to play some old favorites on the shiny piano in the fireside lobby of the retirement home.

Usually he loved playing for her, but tonight his fingers were clumsy and found the wrong keys.

"Something bothering you, Sweet?" she asked him.

He grinned at her nickname for him. "Nothing really."

"There is something," she insisted. "I can tell. You know, I can almost smell it. You've got a guilty conscience."

"You can smell a guilty conscience?" He laughed.

"Yes, a bit. It's a kind of fear, you know, and you might not be able to notice it, but when you're like me and the only things you've really got left are your hearing and sense of smell, they get stronger." She touched his shoulder. "Want to talk about it?"

"Oh," he said, his fingers running lightly across the keyboard, "I committed a sin of omission."

"You didn't tell someone something?"

"That's right, and I should have. It wasn't fair to her either. But my intentions were good."

"Well, you know what my Arthur used to say. The road to you-know-where is paved with good intentions."

"I have no intentions of going to you-know-where," he said, unable to keep the amusement from his voice. "Guess that means I'd better take care of it, right?"

"Well, Sweet," his grandmother said, her thin papery cheeks dimpling with impish delight, "if this involves a woman, I'd say you'd better race to it and get this straightened out."

"If it were a man, I could take my time fixing my mistake, huh?" He couldn't resist teasing her.

"Sweet, there's no doubt in my mind that I have the world's best grandson. I couldn't ask for better than you. But I also want great-grandbabies one of these days. I'm not getting any younger, and neither are you." Her eyes, their brightness only partially dimmed behind thick glasses, followed him as he stood up and got his coat from the rack.

"I'll walk you to your room if you'd like," he offered.

"I'll be okay here. But you've got work to do. Go get her!" She shook a bony fist in the air. "Go now!"

"Yes, Ma'am!"

He was still chuckling as he drove away from Golden Meadows and toward the mall.

Abbey had driven by the sign for Golden Meadows countless times, but she'd never turned down the lane that led to it.

It was, like many retirement communities, near the hospital, but this was tucked back in a grove of trees. What seemed like several buildings were, she realized as she drove up, in fact one large building with connecting halls made primarily of tall, polished windows. On the front door hung a large wreath, its green boughs interwoven with twinkling lights. All in all, it was a bright and cheerful place, not at all like she had imagined it.

The true test would be what the interior was like, she told herself as she parked her car. Inside, it might be the dreadful place she'd imagined it to be.

But as she entered the door, she had to admit that she had been wrong. The front door opened into a great room, the high arched ceiling allowing the biggest Christmas tree she'd ever seen. And it was real. The clean aroma of the large pine tree permeated the air.

"May I help you?" A young woman behind the desk to her right beamed at her.

"It's somewhat hard to explain," Abbey began, suddenly nervous as she put the present on the counter beside her. "You see, I received this gift from my aunt Luellen, who is a dear but a bit on the, well, loopy side. And no big surprise to anyone who knows her, but the present wasn't for me. I don't know who it is for, but maybe you can help me."

"Your aunt Luellen lives here? Are you sure?" the woman asked her, turning toward her computer.

"No, no. Aunt Luellen lives in Brazil right now. She's a missionary."

"How very interesting." The glaze over the young woman's eyes told Abbey that she was perilously close to turning away.

"Let me start again. I have a gift for a woman named Claire. It came from my aunt Luellen. I don't know anyone named Claire, but apparently she lives here, and I'd like to give it to her." Inspiration struck. "Or, I could leave it here, and you could give it to her."

The woman behind the desk pulled back a bit, and her eyes narrowed with faint suspicion. "You want to leave a wrapped parcel for someone you don't know? Oh, I don't think so. It's not our policy to do that."

"Okay, then can you let me know who Claire is, or where she is? I'd like to make sure she gets it, and I do have to get back to work." Abbey glanced at her watch as if to confirm that.

Never taking her eyes off Abbey, the woman dialed a number. "Claire? This is Nadine at the front desk. I have someone here. Her name is—excuse me, what is your name?"

"Abbey Jensen. Tell her I'm Luellen Gregg's niece."

The woman repeated the information into the phone. Her eyebrows rose as she listened to the response. "Are you sure?" she asked.

She paused, then shrugged. "Fine. I'll send her down to your room."

She turned to Abbey. "Room 108. Take the hall on your right, and it's the fourth door down."

Abbey fled the desk and the woman's wary eyes and walked as quickly as she could to the door of room 108. She took a deep breath and knocked.

The door opened to reveal an elderly woman in a wheelchair. Her china blue eyes sparkled behind thick lenses, and she leaned forward a bit, as if to bring Abbey into focus.

"Abbey Jensen? Luellen has talked so much about you, I feel as if I know you! Come in, come in!" She wheeled herself back into her room, motioning Abbey to follow her. "What's Luellen been up to lately?"

"She's still a missionary in Brazil," Abbey said as her eyes took in her surroundings. The room was lovely, done in clean white and bluebonnet blue, and as neat as the proverbial pin. A white porcelain cross hung over a small table on which a Bible was neatly centered. It was bigger than any Bible Abbey had seen, and she realized that it was undoubtedly a large-print edition.

"Brazil? Last I heard it was Chile."

"It probably was Chile, then. I'm pretty bad with keeping up with her."

"Isn't it exciting, though? Traveling through the world, spreading the Word." The old woman's face appeared almost transfixed. "She and I are total opposites of each other. She's the world traveler, and the most I do is go down the hall for dinner."

But rather than sounding sorry for herself, she seemed quite happy.

"By the way, I'm Claire Thorson. Luellen and I have known each other since we were girls. I have a scrapbook I'd love to show you if you have time."

"Actually, I'd love to look at it," Abbey said, amazed that she really would, "but I have to get back to work. I brought your Christmas present from Aunt Luellen. She sent it to me by mistake."

Claire laughed. "Somehow that doesn't surprise me. Luellen was always the one with her head in the clouds, just to be closer to heaven, we used to tease her. I suppose that means I have your gift, then."

She wheeled over to the small tree that was set up by the window and picked up one of the many packages under it. She held it close to her face, trying to read the name.

"Don't worry about it," Abbey reassured her. "It's not that important."

"A Christmas present 'not that important'? My goodness, Abbey Jensen! Yes, it is!"

Abbey grinned at the elderly woman's honesty. Her eagerness about Christmas reminded her of Mike's comment. Christmas mattered quite a bit to Claire. "You're right. It is important, and here is yours." She held out the slippers, now completely rewrapped in bright red foil with a shiny gold bow on the top. "But now I've got to get back to work."

"Where do you work?"

"At the Cedar Mall. I manage Trends."

"Cedar Mall? My grandson works there. Maybe you know him."

"Maybe." Abbey impulsively dropped a kiss on the top of Claire's head. "But I've got to go now."

She opened the door to leave and there, in the hallway, still out of breath from running, stood Mike Tucker.

They all managed to speak at once, and for a moment, chaos reigned supreme. It ended with a sudden blanket of silence as their words settled on them.

"You've met Grandma, I see," Mike said at last.

Before Abbey could say a word, Mike took her by the arm. "Let's go have some coffee," he suggested as he steered her out of Claire's room. "We need to talk."

As they left, Abbey saw Claire lift her hand ever so slightly in a fisted salute. And perhaps her ears were playing tricks on her, but she was sure she heard the older woman whisper, "Wahoo!"

Chapter 3

Mike led Abbey into a small room that opened off the lobby. Several small round tables were clustered near a cozy fireplace, where a hearty fire burned. He poured them each a cup of coffee from the pot on the counter and dropped some change in the pottery piggy bank beside the coffee pot, moving with the easy grace of someone who knew the ropes of Golden Meadows.

A few surprised residents lifted surreptitiously interested glances at them. When he nodded at some of them, smiling and greeting them, Abbey said through closed teeth and a tight smile, "Why don't you introduce me to your friends?"

He nodded at a table of three gentlemen, then sat beside her, sliding a cup toward her. "Because this way you'll be the hit of the rumor mill. They'll all be speculating who Sweet's new girlfriend is."

"Who's Sweet?" she asked, momentarily diverted.

A stain flushed his cheeks with dark color.

"Mike, are you blushing? Well, will you look at that? You are!" She grinned. "Are you Sweet?"

"Yup," he said, ducking his head. "Grandma always said I was the sweetest grandbaby boy in the world, and that soon became Sweet."

"I like it," Abbey said truthfully. "It fits you, in a way. Plus, it's, well, sweet."

Their laughter broke the uneasiness only for a moment. They had serious matters to work out, and Abbey went right to the point. "Mike, why didn't you tell me that your grandmother was Claire?"

His dark eyes were serious when he studied her face. "Would it have mattered?"

"Yes," she replied. "Yes, I think it would have."

"How?"

She thought about her answer before speaking. "Well, I think I would have come out here right away."

"Really?"

Annoyance tinged her response. "Really. I would have at least given it stronger consideration."

He shook his head. "I'm not so sure about that."

"Michael Tucker, I would too have come out here!" she protested, her back straightening. "How can you say such a mean thing about me?"

Mike shifted in his chair. "Let's face it, Abbey. You and I have known each other since we were kids. We never were buddies even when we were children, and the years didn't draw us together; they emphasized our separateness. Your life has been focused on your career."

She tried to interrupt him, but he held up his hand. "Wait. Let me finish. I might as well be hung for a sheep as a lamb, and after all I've said, I'm well on my way to the sheep gallows."

Abbey settled back in her chair, but every nerve in her body tingled with anxious worry. She felt exactly the same way she did during performance evaluations at Trends, knowing that she was about to hear something she didn't want to and that it was unavoidable. The riot in her stomach turned and churned, and she had a fleeting thought that she shouldn't have had the evening special at Pizza Fair.

"We're friends, Mike." She congratulated herself on how even and calm her voice sounded.

"Are we?"

Abbey had heard people say that it felt like their world had been pulled out from under them, but it was a phrase she'd never really understood. But now she did.

"Yes, Mike, we are."

"And who else are your friends?" His words were deadly quiet.

"Well, let's see. There's Brianna and Selma at the store, of course, and, um, then there's Terri. Terri and I have been pals since we were in diapers."

"When did you last see Terri? Talk to her? Write to her?"

"Write to her?" She looked at him blankly.

"Terri moved to Rochester in August," he said gently.

She put her face in her hands. She hadn't known

that. She'd been too busy to call Terri, too busy to drop by, just too busy.

This was terrible, absolutely terrible. The pain was almost too intense to feel. It was as if she were having major surgery—without anesthesia.

A touch on her shoulder startled her. "Is this young man acting like a cad?"

Beside her a thin elderly man balanced on a cane. His hands shook with palsy, and his eyes were murky with cataracts. But his voice was strong, and his meaning was clear as he glared at Mike.

"No, he's fine." She shot a furtive glance at Mike, then looked back at her defender. "He's just offering me some suggestions on how I might improve myself."

Abbey thought the elderly fellow was going to raise his cane and shake it at Mike. But instead, older eyes glared at younger eyes, and the gentleman said, "If there's one thing you should learn, young man, it's that you can't tell a woman anything."

She tried to protest, but he continued, apparently unaware of her interruption. "You can't tell them anything because they know everything. My Eleanor, may she rest in peace, may not have gone past the twelfth grade, but she had a doctorate in Life. Good Christian woman too." The man nodded. "Actually, you can't tell men anything either," he said to Abbey. "It's not because they know everything—they don't— but they've got this problem with their ears."

Abbey was fascinated by this man. "Their ears?"

"Yup. And the fanciest hearing aids in the world can't help with their problem. You can't tell a person anything they don't want to hear, whether they're male or female." He leaned on his cane thoughtfully. "So here I am telling you this, and you probably don't want to hear me either. Go figure. Just because you're old, don't mean you're smart."

"I think that you are extremely smart," Mike declared, "and I'm glad you stopped to talk to us. Right, Abbey?"

"It seems to me that Eleanor got a pretty good deal when she married you," Abbey said softly, suppressing the urge to give the man a hug.

She noticed Mike's quick glance at her as the gentleman walked away. "What?" she snapped.

"You sounded almost like a romantic for a minute there," he said, nearly laughing.

"Yeah, right. Your hearing is pitiful."

"Well, he did say that you only hear what you want to hear," he reminded her.

"And you wanted to hear that I'm a romantic?" She meant it lightly, as a quick and witty response, but as she said it, the meaning struck her.

Mike didn't know it, but his offhand comment— and it was an offhand comment, she was sure—had struck pay dirt. The problem was that this gushy romantic, which she had efficiently buried under the lacquered coat of her career, tended to surface at the most inopportune time, like whenever she watched *Miracle on 34th Street* or when she attended weddings or even when a certain greeting card commercial appeared on television. It was really quite inconvenient.

Hastily, she tried to cover the glimpse of her inner self that had escaped. She changed the subject to something she was more comfortable with: "I've got to get back to work," she announced. "It's late."

Mike glanced at his watch and nodded. "You're right. I'm supposed to meet a friend at Tuck's Toys in fifteen minutes, so I'd better hustle."

She couldn't resist it. "A friend?"

"Yes, Miss Snooper," he answered. "A friend."

"Big friend? Little friend?"

He laughed. "Are you trying to find out if I'm seeing someone? Well, not in that sense, no."

She stood up and busied herself with clearing away her coffee cup. "It's just that you work almost as many hours as I do. I don't even see my mailman, let alone get out to meet people. What do you do? Do you go to the bars after work?"

His expression was half shocked, half amused. "The bars? No, I don't go to the bars. They're not my scene at all. No, my dear, I find my friends at the best place in the world. I find them at church."

"Oh, that," she said dismissively. "They don't count."

He stopped midaction. "Why not?"

"Well, for one thing, they've got to love you. Kind of like parents."

He chuckled. "Not exactly. But in a way you're right. They do have to love you, because Christ told them to."

Abbey responded with a very unladylike snort.

"It's true. Oh, admittedly there are moments when we disagree, but that's just part of it all. That's how we grow."

He was so serious. Mike must take this religion stuff pretty seriously. Of course, his grandmother did too, judging from her room décor.

He took her by the hand. "Abbey, want to come with me to church on Sunday, give it a try?"

"Nah. I need to be at the store early. We're starting our big Christmas promotion that day." For once, she was grateful for the signs and displays that had arrived earlier in the day. She had a ready-made excuse for not going with him.

"There's an early service. You could be out by ten o'clock."

She shook her head. "No, Mike. Thanks for inviting me, but I just don't go for this organized religion stuff."

He grinned. "Well, sometimes we're not so organized at the early service."

"You know what I mean. I believe in God and all that, but this church business is, well, not for me. If I want to say hello to God, I can go to the lake and do it."

"And do you?" His question was quiet and unnerving.

"I've got to get going, Mike." Abbey turned on her heel and left the room before he could say another word.

She fumed all the way back to the mall. Religion was one of those things that people were supposed to keep to themselves.

It was true that Mike had never proselytized. As a matter of fact, this was the first time he'd even mentioned anything having to do with church. But his invitation made her uneasy. And she had to admit that part of the feeling was born of the fact that this opened up another area of Mike that she didn't know existed.

For some reason, she wanted to know more about Mike.

A lot more.

The evening mall traffic had picked up, and Abbey grimaced at the new booths that had gone up since she'd left. The latest one was a peppermint-striped building. Instead of a wall facing the mall corridors, the space was lined with black metal bars.

She edged closer. A large heart-shaped black lock hung on the door.

Abbey couldn't believe her eyes. It looked almost like a jail, but what on earth did a jail have to do with Christmas?

As if in answer to her unspoken question, a workman wearing a Cedar Mall uniform hauled a ladder up to the front of the building. Curiously, she watched as he set up the ladder and climbed it, balancing a large wooden sign. After a few quick taps of his hammer, she had her answer. The sign was lettered in Old West style: "The Candy Cane Calaboose."

"Well," Abbey said to no one in particular, "that explains it." She shook her head. "Or not."

As she started to walk toward Trends, another worker joined the first. The second man carried a sign that was also immediately nailed to the building. She retraced her footsteps and read the new sign: "The mall merchants invite you to watch this spot for holiday fun!"

"Oh, right," she muttered to herself. "Well, not this mall merchant. I wonder what on earth they've decided we're going to have to do now."

She walked back to Trends, mumbling and grumbling about past mall endeavors, such as the potluck when everybody brought desserts and potato salad, and nobody brought a main dish. The mall office had been forced to buy meat and cheese trays from a neighboring grocery store. Then there was the picnic, scheduled for mid-July, prime mosquito season. Even the toughest repellent hadn't been able to repel the hordes of hungry buzzing insects. Next time, Abbey thought, they probably wouldn't have the picnic next to the river. Another one of their grand plans had been a talent show to raise money for a local charity. It soon became apparent that few, if any, of the mall merchants had any talent at all. The talent show had never been repeated, and she thought it was possibly at the charity's request.

No, whatever this Candy Cane Calaboose was, it was going to prove to be an awful idea.

But Abbey hadn't gone to the potluck or the picnic or the talent show anyway. And she had no intention of having anything to do with this latest brainstorm of the mall's management.

She shrugged. This Candy Cane Calaboose nonsense wouldn't bother her one way or the other.

Chapter 4

The alarm went off, and Abbey realized it was aptly named. The little torture device was truly alarming. Every morning its persistent buzz startled her into wakefulness.

She slammed her hand on the snooze button, hoping for a few more precious moments of sleep, but that was a luxury she'd never been able to manage. Once she woke up, she was awake, and there was no going back to sleep for her. Her parents had teased her about her hidden "on" switch.

She missed her parents, especially during the holiday season. But she was a realist. Connecticut might as well be on the other side of the moon this time of year. And they had their own lives, their own friends, and although she knew they'd have been delighted to see her, she also accepted that they were comfortable with their annual summer visits.

It was one of the sacrifices she made for her career, and they understood. The other sacrifice she made for her career was never having a leisurely morning...at least not at Christmas.

As she hurried through her morning routine at a pace that surprised her, she tried not to think about families, the night before, or her visit with Claire. But her thoughts kept returning to Mike and his grandmother.

Somehow it all fit together perfectly, with Aunt Luellen at the center. When things got crazy, her aunt was often the precipitator, with her well-meant actions and her impulsive engineering of situations. She was a kook, that one. Abbey smiled as she thought of what her aunt must be like as a missionary. What on earth did the people of Brazil—or wherever she was—think of her version of the gospel? She could only imagine how it would come out through the filter of Aunt Luellen's nutty brain.

Abbey gasped with surprise as her feet touched the linoleum of her kitchen. It was icy cold. Slippers. She needed to get some slippers. She was on the verge of making a mental note to buy some at the mall when the irony of it all struck her.

She could have had slippers—goofy frog slippers. At least Claire's toes should be toasty warm after Christmas.

That reminded her. She had to get out to see Claire and retrieve the package that Aunt Luellen had sent. That is, she corrected herself, if it were for her. Knowing Aunt Luellen, she might have her entire Christmas gift list scrambled beyond repair. The gift that Claire had could easily be a fishing rod meant for Uncle Kirby in Oregon.

But the sooner she got out there and straightened this whole mishmash out, the sooner she could get back to her own life again and shrug off this crazy business. Her conversation with Mike was still making her uncomfortable, and she didn't like to be uncomfortable.

She snatched her purse from the hook by the door and headed out into the cold. Yes, if she was ever going to have peace of mind, she was going to have to get this thing taken care of once and for all.

Her car groaned into life, and Abbey shivered as she sat in her driveway, waiting for the engine to warm up. There wasn't any new snow, and the sky was a bright, clear blue, but that didn't mean anything when it came to the temperature. It had to be below zero.

She glanced at the spot where an indoor/outdoor thermometer had been attached to her house, but it had fallen off during a late autumn windstorm, and she just hadn't had the chance to put it back up. Then she remembered: The thermometer had fallen off during the autumn of last year. She was really letting things slide.

Well, she countered as she continued her discussion with herself, it wasn't as if she had time. She was busy at the store...and looking into maybe going back to school...and life was just generally hectic. It was something she'd come to live with.

She rubbed her hands together. Even through her thick mittens—on sale at Trends, two pairs for eight dollars—the icy air pierced right to her bones. The defroster had cleared only a small section of her frosty windshield, and she impatiently turned on the wipers, hoping to hurry the process along. She did not want to get out and scrape the window off. It was just too cold.

But the windshield began to film up on the inside from the warmth of her body, so she knew she was in for a wait, and she was too edgy to sit in her car and wait patiently. She fidgeted with the wipers, monkeyed with the defroster, and tried to rub the frost off with her mittened hand, succeeding only in smearing the fog. At last the windshield was clear enough, and she headed off.

This was going to be quick, she promised herself. She'd run in, pick up the present from Claire, say a few bland and polite words, and be on her way. Five minutes, tops. And she'd be through with this whole bizarre slippers thing and able to get on with her life.

Whatever that might be, a nagging little voice whispered in her heart.

Mike? Surely, Mike didn't have anything to do with her life. He was just a friend—or not a friend, she thought as she remembered their conversation. It made her stomach hurt.

She pulled into a spot near the door of Golden Meadows. The tall windows sparkled in the morning light. From the parking lot, she could see the mammoth Christmas tree through the largest windows in the entryway. The lights were on, catching the sunlit crystals of ice on the edges of the windows. With the early morning frost lit by the tree lights' multicolored array, the building looked incredibly picturesque.

She briefly considered leaving the car running but decided against it. She was already low on fuel and about the last thing she needed now was to run out of gas in the parking lot of a retirement community. So she switched off the ignition, telling herself she'd be inside such a short time that the car would still be warm—or warmish—when she came out again.

Resolutely, she marched into the high-arched lobby of Golden Meadows and approached the desk. Just her luck. The same woman who'd been there earlier was there again. Nadine, that was her name.

"Yes?" It was remarkable, truly remarkable, how much iciness the woman could pack into the single word.

"I'd like to see Claire. Claire Thorson."

"Is she expecting you?"

"Yes. No. She is, but probably not right this minute. I mean, she knows I'm coming, but not necessarily today. Well, really, she's not expecting me at all right now, since it's opening time at the mall and it's Christmas."

The woman behind the desk stared at her, her expression never wavering. What was it about her that made Abbey splutter and blither like this?

"You're the lady with the package," Nadine said at last.

Abbey nodded, unsure of what the woman was going to do.

She certainly didn't expect this: Nadine burst into a huge smile and leaned across the desk to capture Abbey's hands. "Thank you so much for bringing the gift to her. You know, Mike's pretty much the only family she's got here anymore, and while he is here daily, bless his heart, having a new young face in her life has meant so much. She's really perked up."

Abbey could feel the smile freezing on her face as the woman continued to gush. "I hope you'll be back more often. This is just doing her a world of good." Then the woman delivered the *coup de grace*. "Plus you're almost family."

"Almost family?" Abbey gulped.

"You and her grandson, Mike. You're, well, you know." Nadine stopped just short of a conspiratorial wink.

"We're what?" Abbey asked through nearly numb lips. "No, never mind. I have the feeling this is something I don't want to hear." She shot a wild smile at the receptionist. "So, is Claire in her room?"

"No, Honey. She's with the others, down in the Fireside Lounge. You can go ahead. It's just down this hall, take a left, then a quick right. You can't miss it. There's a fireplace the size of a Buick in there. And they're all in there singing their dear hearts out, so follow the music."

Abbey felt her face relax. Maybe she could make it through this after all. She started down the hall, and she could just make out the sound of voices raised in song. They finished the last triumphant notes of a hymn Abbey somewhat recognized and, after some murmured discussion, a series of chords led them into another song.

What the group lacked in talent, they made up for in enthusiasm. Some voices were quavering with age; others were strong and true, undiminished by the years. One clear tenor led them all. She knew even before she peeked around the corner who the voice belonged to. He motioned her in as he kept on lead-ing the group in singing.

If only the song hadn't been a rather rousing rendi-tion of "When the Saints Come Marchin' In." Abbey's face flooded with red when the audience's singing lagged as they turned around to stare at her with open curiosity. The voices faded out as the residents stud-ied the newcomer.

She tried to cover her embarrassment by whisper-ing loudly to an elderly gentleman in the back row: "I'm not a saint, and I'm not marching."

To her chagrin, he leaned back and said, just as loudly, "Could have been worse. The song before last was 'How Great Thou Art.'"

She knew she shouldn't, that she would be doomed if she did. But she couldn't help it. She looked at Mike.

His face was as red as hers but with suppressed amusement. As their eyes met, Abbey and Mike dis-solved into laughter. It wasn't the genteel, tee-hee, hymn-sing kind of laughter either. Oh, no. It was the can't-catch-your-breath, clutch-your-sides, gulp-and-snort brand of laughter that takes over and won't let go.

Tears ran down her face, and she collapsed onto the nearest folding chair and wiped her eyes as she tried to control herself. The harder she tried, the worse she laughed.

Just when she thought she had mastered her laugh attack, she looked at Mike. His attempt to look as sober failed as their glances locked again, and once more they both gave way to the laughter.

"Hmmph!" A man in a plaid shirt settled himself into a posture of righteous indignation. "Such behavior! Have you ever witnessed such a scene in your life? This is a hymn sing, not a vaudeville show. They ought to—"

"Get married," a tiny lady with a lace scarf finished for him. She sighed happily. "Get married and have lots of little Sweets."

Abbey stopped midgulp. The woman's voice carried clearly through the room, and from the way that Mike froze in place, bent at a nearly impossible angle, she knew he had heard her. His hand was motionless on the strings of his guitar, and if she didn't know better, she'd think he was a wax figure from Madame Tussaud's.

Lots of little Sweets?

Mike was staring at her, looking at her with a strangled pain she knew mirrored her own shock. She knew she should get up and leave, but her muscles were apparently cemented into place. Dimly she heard sounds behind her, and a familiar tinkling giggle broke the silence. "Speaking of Sweet, how about 'Sweet Hour of Prayer'? Come on, everybody! I love that hymn. I'll start." Claire's wavering but true soprano started the hymn, and the others soon joined in.

Abbey could have kissed her as the crowd faced forward again. Mike, after a split-second pause to collect himself, joined in with his guitar.

As soon as the attention had turned from her, Abbey decided, she'd leave. She'd creep out, hoping no one would notice. She'd deal with the wayward Christmas gift later. She had to get back to the mall. Her fingers pushed back her sleeve, and she grimaced. She'd forgotten to put on her watch.

Surreptitiously she glanced around the room, trying to find a clock. Surely there'd be one on the fireplace. But nothing. There were no clocks in the room at all. Maybe, she thought, when you got to this point in life, time didn't matter. You just moved from Activity A to Activity B to lunch, then rested, then Activity C, Activity D, dinner, television, and to bed. She resisted the urge to shudder. This was definitely not the life for her.

The woman with the lace collar leaned over to her. "Need the time?" she asked as she held her thin wrist over toward Abbey.

Abbey realized she was the only person in the room without a watch on. That might explain the dearth of clocks. Golden Meadows supplied the activities, but each resident was responsible for his or her own time.

Maybe that was what Aunt Luellen was talking about. Maybe this was what rejoicing in the day meant.

She smiled at the woman with the watch. The group had begun another song, a Christmas carol. She should leave, but this was "Joy to the World." It had been her favorite when she was a child, and she couldn't resist joining in as the words came back easily to her mind.

She'd stay for this one song, and that was it. How long could a song take? A minute, two tops, right? She'd allow herself the luxury of one song, then she had to get to work.

But the lure of the familiar carols soon wrapped their magic around her, and she stayed for "He Is Born" and "Hark, the Herald Angels Sing." As the last note drifted into silence, she glanced at her neighbor's watch.

It was a few minutes after ten!

Trends was already open! She scooped up her purse and made a hasty, muted farewell to the members of the hymn sing and raced out the door, down the hall, past a surprised Nadine, and into the cold clear air of a Minnesota morning.

It wasn't as if no one was at Trends to open it. Selma was scheduled to be there at eight-thirty, and she was so reliable that Abbey knew she was there by eight-fifteen. But Abbey needed to be at the mall, at Trends.

Actually, what she needed was to be away from here, away from Golden Meadows and this whole bizarre scene with Mike. And away from all those hymns. Her mind swam with the memories of long-neglected melodies, and the words came back to haunt her. It was amazing how easily they sprang back into her mind, although it had been years since she'd set foot inside a church.

The carols, of course, she'd heard every minute of every hour of every day since November fifth, the official start of the holiday season at the mall. She could sing them in her sleep. Abbey snorted. She probably did sing them in her sleep.

She snapped her attention back to the road as a patch of ice nearly sent her car spinning off the paved parking lot. Now there was a metaphor she could understand: Be in control. Hold the steering wheel tightly and never take your eyes off the road ahead, and you will stay directed. For her, that meant staying on track, straight toward her MBA and a real career with megabucks in her bank account. If she kept her target in sight, as she had been, she'd stay on the path to her heart's treasure.

Somewhere in the back of her mind, she could hear Aunt Luellen saying something about heart's treasure. Abbey shrugged. If it were Aunt Luellen, it was undoubtedly something from the Bible.

She'd had her dose of religion for the day. A couple of rousing Christmas carols, and look at her. She was wrapped in that soft-focus, greeting-card kind of glow that retailers relied on to pull them through the Christmas season.

There were Christian retailers, she was sure, who looked upon the season as a time to celebrate Jesus' birth. But there were just as many, if not more, who saw this as a season of profits, and a tiny baby born in a stable played only a minor part in it. The thought saddened her, even though she wasn't a dyed-in-the-wool Christian like Aunt Luellen.

Christmas was the base of the retailer's year. It was what carried them though the lean times in other months and kept them going. Without Christmas to boost their sales, many stores would not be able to stay in business. And now that she was a store manager, she was part of the feeding frenzy when it came to Christmas. She had to be. She had a responsibility to the storeowners and the other employees. Abbey sighed and pushed away the thoughts that jostled around in her mind, arguing with each other. Why did Christmas have to be so complicated?

She pulled out of the Golden Meadows parking area and into the stream of traffic, trying to squish the not-so-tiny voice that insisted she didn't believe a word she was thinking—that Christmas was a time of holiness and joy, and that stores like Trends played only the most minor of roles in its celebration.

The wise men may have brought the newborn Jesus gifts of incomparable value, but somehow she didn't think they would have shopped at the Cedar Mall, with "forty-two individual stores offering the region's widest assortment of shopping pleasure," as the television commercial boasted.

As if on cue, she could hear Aunt Luellen's voice from many childhood Christmases: "The greatest gift of all was not what they brought Him but what He brought us."

Abbey sighed. That was true. What was a television set compared to everlasting life?

Or a pair of goofily grinning frog slippers?

Chapter 5

The mall was already filling with customers, even though it had been open less than an hour. Selma was busily refreshing the stock from one of the cartons that seemed to arrive every hour, although Abbey knew deliveries were only twice a day.

"Hey, Stranger, good to see you! Don't tell me you overslept!" Her clerk grinned at her.

"Ha. I don't even sleep, so oversleeping is too much to ask for." Abbey said it lightly, but the weariness that seeped into her bones told her that her words weren't that far from the truth.

"No kidding. One of these days you'll have to try sleeping. It's vastly underrated, at least in your world," Selma commented wryly.

"After Christmas. Then I'll have time."

Selma snorted inelegantly. "After Christmas come the returns, then it's Valentine's Day, then…"

"Okay, I'll take a Wednesday off sometime and try sleeping."

"Wednesdays are Senior Citizens days here, remember?"

Abbey made a face at her salesclerk. "Whatever. I'm too tired to argue." Their eyes met, and both women laughed.

"Okay, lecture ended. Now, where do you want these?" Selma handed Abbey a box of brightly colored slipper socks, and Abbey gasped.

She'd gone all the way out to Golden Meadows to pick up the gift, but she'd left without it. She slammed her fist down on the counter.

"Okay," Selma said, drawing the two syllables out. "What just took you from mellow to mad?"

"These slippers."

In one smooth movement, Selma reached out, took the box, and tossed it under the counter, then smiled innocently at her boss. "What slippers?"

"No, no," Abbey responded with a frustrated sigh. "They just reminded me that I was supposed to pick something up, and I forgot. Now I have to go back, and I don't really want to."

Selma knelt to get the box again. "Anything I can do to help?" Her voice was muffled from under the counter.

Now there was an idea! Selma could go to Golden Meadows…. But before the thought took full root, Abbey dismissed it. She had to see this through to the end.

"No, I'm just busily berating myself. For some reason I can't seem to remember to pick up the gift my aunt Luellen sent to Golden Meadows."

"She sent your Christmas present to Golden Meadows? Isn't that a retirement home?" Selma threw back her head and roared with laughter. "Honey, I think your auntie is trying to tell you something!"

"You are not even a little bit funny," Abbey responded, although she had to smile. "All I need is a simple brain transplant, and I'll be fine."

"Would that be out-patient surgery?" Selma ducked the teasing swipe Abbey gave her.

The two spent the rest of the day companionably unpacking new arrivals and setting up the merchandise. As soon as they emptied one box, another arrived to take its place, or so it seemed. Between the two of them, they barely made a dent in the towering stacks of cardboard boxes, all marked "URGENT: OPEN FIRST."

"I'm here!" The voice of the college student who worked part-time called to them from the front of the store.

"Hi, Brianna." Abbey groaned as she rose from the crouched position where she'd been retrieving an entire boxed shipment of rings that had broken open a few moments ago. Rings had rolled all over the store, coming to rest in the most difficult-to-reach positions. "What are you doing here so early?"

"Early?" Brianna looked confused. "I'm here to work. I'm supposed to be here at five, aren't I?"

Abbey and Selma exchanged glances. Selma said affectionately, "Yes, dear, but it's only—" She consulted her watch and gasped. "It's nearly five!"

"No wonder I'm so hungry. Selma, you can go on

home, and Brianna, if you'll straighten that holiday sweatshirt display, I'll—"

"Get something to eat." Selma pushed Abbey toward the front of the store. "You haven't even had lunch, and I suspect you skipped breakfast too. I'm on for another hour anyway, and Brianna and I can certainly cover long enough for you to get a decent meal."

Abbey opened her mouth to object when a familiar voice spoke from behind her.

"I'll take care of it, Selma. Come on, Abbey, let's go get some grub." Mike grinned at her.

"Some grub?" Brianna laughed out loud. "Man, you've got to do something about your romantic style."

It seemed to Abbey that everyone began to speak at once, and the mayhem ended only when she was unceremoniously shoved outside the open gate of Trends, her coat in her hands, with Mike laughing at her side.

"I think we're going out to dinner," he said at last.

"I don't need my coat for that. Actually, I don't need dinner at all but—" As if on cue, her stomach rumbled loudly.

"The case of the tattletale tummy," Mike said. "Let's go."

"Just let me put my coat back. We can run down to the pretzel place and grab a stuffed pretzel and a soda."

He put his hand on her arm. "No pretzels. We're going to go out for a real dinner."

"A real meal?" A terrible thought struck her. He

had said that he often ate with his grandmother. "Oh, no, Mike. We're not going to eat at Golden Meadows."

He shook his head. "No, but I do go out there sometimes to eat with Grandma. I like to do that."

She shuddered. "I don't mean to be horrid, but I can't imagine that being anything you'd want to do."

"Well, I like it. But that's not where we're going tonight. We're going to a real restaurant, the kind where you sit down, they hand you a menu, you get a salad and a meal with vegetables. And maybe a dessert that doesn't come wrapped in plastic."

It did sound good. So Abbey allowed herself to be ushered through the icy-cold parking lot, then driven to a nearby family restaurant, Ginger's. The restaurant's brick-and-glass exterior was softened by chintz curtains and tablecloths, and Abbey detected the warm inviting scent of meatloaf. She had to admit it: this was a great idea. She was starving.

"This must be new. I've never been in here before," she said as she sipped the water the waitress handed her.

Mike shot her a curious look. "It's been here about a year and a half. I'd ask where you've been, but I know—working."

"That's not really fair," Abbey protested. "It's not like I don't have any life at all outside Trends."

Mike smiled ruefully. "I'm sorry. It came out sounding harsher by far than I intended. It's just that it's been true of me. I realized that my whole life was revolving around work. I'm trying to cut back a bit."

Abbey couldn't help it. She laughed. "You're cutting back? That's ludicrous."

He seemed surprised. "Why do you say that? I don't work nearly as many hours as you do."

"Who was the only person besides me at the mall at eleven o'clock at night when I got locked out of the store? You. Mike Tucker. Workaholic."

He had the grace to look abashed. "That's true. But I am trying to do better. Like not grabbing a hot dog or a pretzel in the evening and calling it dinner."

"We're busy, Mike," she said in her own defense— their own defense. "It's not like we have the time to do full-course meals."

"We don't? I don't know about you, but I've been neglecting myself lately."

"Neglecting yourself?"

"I know. Sounds kind of selfish, doesn't it? But I'm starting to realize that I've got to take care of my body. And that includes eating right as well as getting some exercise."

Abbey glanced at him suspiciously. "Are you one of those exercise fanatics?"

He struck an exaggerated muscle-man pose. "I'm in the running for Mr. America, hadn't you noticed?" He laughed, and for the first time she noticed that he had dimples. Actually, very cute dimples. The kind that made his eyes light up like— She broke off that train of thought before it could go further.

He was still talking, and she pulled her attention back to his words. "So I promised myself that one day I'll join a gym, and I will, but right now if I can make a turn around the mall with the other mall walkers, I consider it my exercise for the day. No, right now I'm aiming for some sleep and some veggies. Baby steps first."

The waitress appeared with their coffee. "You ready to order?"

Her words took Abbey by surprise. She hadn't even looked at the menu. "What do you recommend?" she asked Mike.

"They have really good soup," he said.

Soup sounded wonderful. Nice and warm and filling, the perfect food for a cold December evening.

"I'll be right out with the bread," the server said as she collected their menus and left.

"We get a loaf of homemade bread with flavored butter. It comes with our meal," Mike said. "It's just this side of heaven."

"I haven't had homemade bread in years," Abbey commented. "Not since Mom made it, and that has to be, wow, four years ago? They've been gone that long?"

Mike's forehead wrinkled with concern, and it took Abbey a moment to realize why. "Oh, I didn't mean that kind of gone, I meant gone as in gone from Minnesota. They live in Connecticut now. Dad was transferred just shortly after I graduated from high school. I guess that's something you wouldn't have known."

He nodded. "Probably. Are you going to go out there for Christmas?"

"No." For the first time since she and her parents had been separated, she felt a twinge at being apart from them at the holidays, but she quickly suppressed it. "That's okay. We've only got Christmas Day off anyway. It's not worth it. What about you?"

"Well, Dad passed on last year."

Abbey felt herself flush. "Oh, I'm sorry. I didn't

know. What a horrible thing to bring up at this time of year."

"It's certainly true I miss him, but I miss him every day of the year. It's still raw, and it hurts, but I know he's celebrating Christmas in heaven." He smiled contemplatively. "To be honest, that's what gets me through. I know you might not believe it, but it's enough."

His words took her by surprise, and her expression must have mirrored her feelings, because he continued, "I'm not saying that those first days didn't hurt with a pain as if someone had cut my heart right out of my chest, but my faith is strong, and his faith was stronger. He taught me that this life is great…and the next life is going to be even greater."

"How about your mother?" Abbey wanted to change the subject. She was in no mood for the turn the conversation was taking. She didn't want to think about things like religion, at least not now. She wanted to relax.

It wasn't that she didn't believe, not really. She did. She just didn't have the time to reason it all out. One of these days she would, when she had time.

Mike didn't seem to be bothered by her lack of interest in his family's faith. "Mom moved to Arizona, and she lives with her sister in a mobile home where she can reach out her bedroom window and pick an orange for breakfast. She says she doesn't care if she never sees another snowflake."

"So she's not coming up here for Christmas?"

He shook his head. "No. I won't get to see her at all this Christmas, sad to say. I have to stay here because of the store. This is the worst time of year for a toy store owner to take a vacation."

Abbey smiled. "I suppose you're right. It's the price you pay for owning your own store."

"Keep that in mind, Abbey, in case you decide to trade in managing for ownership. But I'll pop down there in February and visit. Right about then I figure I'll really need a blast of warmth. It'll be interesting to see what she thinks about celebrating Christmas in the desert."

"Arizona is a real change from Minnesota," Abbey commented. "I don't know if I could do it. I need snow and sweaters and mittens for it to be Christmas."

"I know what you mean," he agreed. "But there are times when I think I'd really like to try a Christmas without snow." He shivered. "Like last night. Did you hear how cold it got? Can you imagine what it must have been like to live here before electricity?"

"I remember reading about how people used to live in sod houses," Abbey said. "First off, I can't for a minute imagine what that was like." She shuddered. "Living in a house made of dirt? And what was it like to heat it by a stove? I'm glad to have my house, that's for sure."

"And my coffeemaker," Mike added, with a wry grin. "These cold mornings, I think I take all that for granted."

Their food arrived, but they barely noticed it, chatting companionably about the blessings of modern appliances, especially furnaces. All too soon, the soup was gone, the coffee cups drained, and Mike leaned back and rubbed his stomach. "I don't know about you, but I'm stuffed. We'd better get back."

They'd talked about nothing, but at the same time they'd talked about everything. Abbey thought that over as they rode in the comfortable dark cocoon of Mike's car. Somehow she felt she knew Mike better, but how on earth had that happened? The most personal their conversation had gotten was about their parents and where they lived now. Hardly the kind of thing that would qualify as an innermost secret. But now she felt closer to him.

And, she realized with surprise, she liked him. She really liked him.

He pulled into the snowy stretches of the mall's parking lot. As she opened the door on her side of the car, he pulled on the handle from the outside. Suddenly their faces were only inches from each other, and the strangest thing happened. Her mouth poised for his kiss, and she felt herself leaning in toward him, as if it were the most natural thing in the world.

Abbey hadn't had much experience with romance. Her knowledge was pretty much limited to some clandestine smooching behind the school with Edwin Carlson when she was fourteen. But she'd heard that a really good fellow and a really good kiss would sweep her off her feet.

Apparently it was true. She felt her feet leave the ground, as though she were floating, while Mike's arms grasped her shoulders, then her waist with a fervent intensity. The world spun around in a dizzying whirl, and the stars arched overhead.

"Aaaaaaabbey!" His voice echoed in her ears as they ascended quickly and just as rapidly descended.

Whomp!

With a very definite thump, she landed on the ground in an inelegant sprawl, with Mike nearby. Her long skirt was tangled in the heels of her boots, and her hat had slipped over one eye. Her bright yellow mittens were now smudged with black where she'd tried to stop her fall. The contents of her purse had escaped, and a lipstick was still skittering across the pavement.

"Are you okay, Abbey?" Mike said. "Wow, this parking lot is icy."

Her hip ached, and her arm, she knew, was going to sport a livid bruise in the morning. But it was nothing compared to her crushed ego.

This was why she had never been a ballerina, why she had never been chosen as a cheerleader. She had all the grace of a lumbering orangutan. She looked as if she should be a dancer, with her slender build, but somewhere between her brain and her feet, the message got scrambled. She was such a klutz. Mike undoubtedly thought she was clumsy, to the point of being dangerous to those standing near her, but what worried her most was something else.

Had she really wanted Mike to kiss her? What on earth had she been thinking of? And worse, what if she hadn't slipped? What if she had actually leaned in too far and kissed him?

He probably would have pulled away, and that would have been the end of their rapidly developing friendship.

Did he know she had been leaning in for his kiss? And if he did, did he think that she was forward, that she did this with anybody who took her to dinner?

Being a recluse floating on an iceberg in the middle of the Atlantic Ocean was looking better by the minute.

Mike cradled his head in his hands. He'd never been the most graceful gazelle in the herd, that was a given, but tonight he'd really blown it. He'd been about to kiss her and had lost his bearings completely.

He had wanted to kiss her so badly that he'd lost whatever moral compass he had. He wasn't the kind of fellow to just kiss a woman because she was pretty, or because he'd had a good time being with her, or anything like that. No, for him a kiss was serious business.

That is, it was until his fancy footwork took them both down in a mall parking lot. The memory made him cringe. She must think he was a total idiot, or at least a complete clumsy Charlie. The next time he was going to get carried away by the moonlight, he'd make sure he wasn't standing on a patch of ice.

Chapter 6

Abbey woke up the next morning feeling a mixture of contentment and annoyance. She had enjoyed dinner far beyond what she'd expected. It was the kind of thing she could get used to…as long as she had someone to eat with.

Someone like Mike? a little voice nagged.

She'd known Mike since they were children. All through their teen years, when everybody of the opposite gender was a potential love interest, she had never thought of him in that sense, and she was sure the thought of going out with her had never crossed his mind either.

Not that it mattered. Even if she were attracted to him—which she wasn't—last night certainly made it clear that he saw her as a friend. A klutzy friend.

She mulled it over as she waited for her curling

iron to heat. Although Mike had been ever-the-gentleman and helped her up, even retrieved her wayward lipstick from under a car where it had rolled and at last come to rest, he had to be wondering about her. What kind of woman would try to kiss somebody in a parking lot, then lose her balance in the process?

Could she be any more out of practice?

She hastily dismissed the thought. For one thing, she was perfectly capable of doing anything she wanted to do. If she'd wanted to make their dinner date an evening to remember, she certainly could have done so. She stood straighter and glared at her mirrored reflection. Yes, she could have knocked his proverbial socks right off.

The truth was, she had come really close. She'd knocked his hat off.

The image in the mirror glared back at her and reminded her of one important element that she was overlooking in this conversation with herself: this developing romance that she sometimes felt and sometimes didn't was completely one-sided. Mike was only trying to be her friend.

That brought her back to the second part of her morning thoughts. It hadn't been a date. Not even close. It had simply been two friends having dinner together.

Friends. The conversation at Golden Meadows sprang back into her mind, and for a moment Abbey felt uneasy. Maybe she—

She shook her head. No. She was fine. Just fine. All she had to do was quit mooning at the mirror like a lunatic and get going, or she was going to be an unemployed lunatic.

A light snow had fallen during the night, and while it made the main road to the mall a pleasant seasonal white, it also made it a crazy ride. The slicked roads forced her to drive slowly, because the fairly simple act of braking to a stop took at least half a block.

A blue four-wheel drive vehicle passed her, able to go faster because it had greater traction than her small car had. She glanced at it, then did a double take.

It was Mike's car, and by the way he was tapping his fingers on the steering wheel and moving his lips, she figured he must be singing along with the radio.

She didn't have time to react emotionally. She'd taken her eyes off the road just long enough to lose control. With a sick sensation in the base of her stomach, she tried futilely to bring her car out of its slide and back into the line of traffic.

"Don't let me hit someone," she said, and she didn't worry about who she was talking to. The message was more important.

The sensation of having her car skid, the steering wheel useless in her hands, was horrible. Then she saw a child walking on the sidewalk, completely absorbed in sliding on the slick pavement, gliding along as if he were ice-skating. The scream that rose in her throat died as her car slid sideways and launched itself, neatly and totally, into a snow bank, a few yards from the little boy.

She popped open the door of her car. As completely wedged in as she was, she could get it ajar just a few inches. "Are you okay?" she called to the boy, but he continued to skate on, the muffler and hat that covered his ears apparently preventing him from hearing her.

"Thank God," she breathed. That had been entirely too close.

The boy was all right. Now she had to get to the business of getting her car out of the snow. She drove into the snowdrift, she told herself, so logically she should be able to drive out again.

After futilely switching gears between reverse and drive, she gave up. She had two options. One, she could call the neighboring gas station to come and get her out. But who knew when they'd get there, and she could guess at how much that call would cost her. Or she could go directly to the second option. It was free. It was the shovel in her trunk.

The first challenge was getting the door open. It would only open about six inches before the snowdrift stopped it. She was thin, but not that thin.

How could she dig herself out when she was trapped inside the car?

Finally she settled on a successful combination of digging with her hand for awhile, then slamming the door open, and repeating the motion. Dig, slam. Dig, slam. Dig, slam. At last it worked, and she was able to escape from her car.

Her success was limited, however. She was still in the snow bank.

Abbey clambered across the snowdrift, wincing as a soft patch of it gave way, and her foot slid up to her knee in the icy crystals. The sharp pain from her hip as her leg turned reminded her of her elegant fall in the parking lot the night before. She opened the trunk, taking care not to drop her keys in the snow, and got the shovel.

She began digging the compressed snow from

under her car. Her long scarf, which she'd purchased for its color rather than its utility, was much too long and slid down from the bottom of her face and hung loosely. After the fourth time that it got caught in the shovel and nearly decapitated her, she yanked it off and threw it aside in disgust.

Her nose was running, and she was sure that her hair looked like elves lived in it. Somehow, she knew, Mike Tucker was to blame for this.

Mike whistled as he raised the grating that covered the entrance to Tuck's. He ducked under it, and as he turned the key to lower it again, he smiled to himself.

You've given me a good year, Lord, he prayed silently as he always did while he went about the opening process. He was in the store by himself, and it was a good time to visit with God. It wasn't his only time of prayer, but even though it was informal, he found it to be valuable preparation for the day—and he was able to focus more clearly for evening prayers.

He continued to talk to God as he restocked the displays, started up the tills, and dusted off the countertop. *The store is doing well, Grandma is settling in just fine at Golden Meadows, and my mother is adjusting to living without Dad in Arizona. Thank You for the blessings You've given me.*

Two thoughts popped into his prayers simultaneously. The first was simple: *How can I repay You?* The second was complex: *Watch over Abbey Jensen and touch her heart to open it for You. She needs You so much.*

Even as he prayed the words, he knew what was

being asked of him. The second thought was the answer to the first.

Aw, God. I meant for You to watch over her. Not me. I'm not good at that. He paused and straightened an already straight display. *Here's a suggestion: How about if I serve on another committee at church instead?*

Silence. Not that he had expected God to answer him aloud. He could always feel the response in his soul. God wasn't a bargainer, he knew that, but maybe he just hadn't offered the right bait.

No, huh? Okay, I'll increase my giving at church. Surely You can't argue with that.

God didn't argue, but that resounding emptiness stayed hollow, and Mike had to accept the truth: God wanted him to do what he could to point Abbey toward God.

He thought about it as he went through his workday. He didn't want to get involved romantically with Abbey. It wasn't that he didn't like her—he did. Oh, as a friend, he hastily told himself. And he'd enjoyed their time together. But he certainly didn't want to get involved with her as deeply as he thought God was asking him to.

Besides, he could imagine what Abbey would say if he started hanging around her, watching over her both physically and spiritually. He laughed. *Are you sure about this, God?*

Well, he'd give it a try. The warm, loving glow that came over him told him that this was the right thing to do.

Caring for Abbey… He had to admit, the thought had its appeal.

* * *

Thanks to having stuck her car in the snow pile, Abbey had pulled into the parking lot with only moments to spare before Trends opened.

Usually, her lateness would have made her tense—even more so after her unfortunate experience with her car—but today she welcomed the diversion. The morning scurry to have the tills ready by the time the front gate came up was intensified, and she was glad to see an early morning crowd already window-shopping in preparation for the stores to open.

"Honey, you look like you've been at hard labor," Selma said as Abbey rushed to have the store in perfect condition by opening time.

"That's not far from the truth," Abbey said. "A snow bank and I had a disagreement."

Selma clucked sympathetically. "'Tis the season, that's for sure. The roads were in pitiful shape this morning, weren't they? I almost got to meet the fella down the street. You know I've been wanting to run into him sometime to introduce myself. Well, this morning I almost got my chance. In fact, I nearly ran him down when my car went out of control on an ice patch."

They chuckled. Selma's romantic life was a constant trial to her. She had more boyfriends than Abbey had been able to keep track of, but none of them seemed to materialize into husband material.

Selma got a sly look in her eye and asked with clearly faked casualness, "So how did it go last night?"

Abbey diverted her eyes and attentively arranged

the Christmas jewelry display. "Last night? Oh, that's right. It was fine."

"Fine? That's all you have to say? Fine?"

"Okay, 'fine' may not be the best word to describe it. It was great."

Selma smiled happily and settled back onto the chair behind the cash register. "Now we're talking! Did anything exciting happen?"

"As a matter of fact, it did. Something totally unexpected, and I was soooo glad." Abbey couldn't resist baiting Selma.

Selma's eyes got huge. "What? What?"

Abbey took a deep breath, then said melodramatically, "We went to Ginger's. I'd never been there before. They have good soup."

For a moment, she thought Selma might explode. "Never mind the soup. I want details. Give me details."

"You want details? What kind of details?"

"Boy details. Girl details."

"There are no details," Abbey said, bringing the conversation to an end. "The best part of the evening was the soup."

As she walked to the front of the store, she was sure she heard Selma mutter something under her breath that sounded not very nice.

Abbey raised the gate to the store, and a handful of customers wandered in. Those early customers got her total attention, and soon the conversation with Selma was ancient history in her mind. After all, the last thing she wanted to think about today was dinner last night with Mike.

* * *

"Want me to get the mail?" Selma asked awhile later. "It's almost noon. It should be here by now."

"Why don't I do it, then you can take the first lunch shift," Abbey suggested. "I could use a break, and so could you."

"I'd argue," Selma said, "but I wonder if part of the reason for your decision is the chance that you might meet a certain toy store owner at the mailboxes."

Abbey didn't answer, partially because she knew Selma was teasing, but also because her assistant was right on the mark.

The mall mailboxes were clustered at the end of a service entrance on the opposite side of the mall, and all shop owners and managers watched for the mail arrival carefully, especially this time of year, when the pace of sales picked up in the afternoon. If she didn't get the mail now, it would be early evening before she'd have a chance to do so.

It was something all the managers knew, so between eleven-thirty and noon, they tended to cluster down there and spend a few minutes sharing quick updates—and extensive gossip.

She could hear them laughing even before turning the corner to the service entrance. From the words that floated free of the general chaotic noise, she realized that the topic of conversation had something to do with a recent decision of mall management.

She slipped through the cluster of kiosks that broke the traffic pattern—when had that fireplace mini-store gone in?—and made her way to the mailboxes. The trip usually took her under five minutes, but now, thanks to the displays the mall management had put up, she had to run an obstacle course.

The managers motioned her into their group, and one of the women handed her a flyer. "Get this," she said to Abbey. "Honestly, what this new executive outfit won't do!"

"I've heard of stupid ideas, but this takes the cake!" added another.

"What's going on?" Abbey asked the woman who had handed her the flyer. "What have they done now?"

The woman just shook her head and threw her copy of the flyer into the nearby recycling bin. "You don't want to know. Oh, you've got one of their notices. Read it for yourself. I, for one, don't have time for this kind of nonsense. If they want to help the retailers, they could hire some extra help. But not this. The last thing I need is to be taken off the floor at Christmas!"

"Those people who come up with these ideas must have fruitcake for brains," another woman chimed in.

"Or reindeer tap-dancing on their heads," someone else agreed. "This idea is downright idiotic."

"Careful what you say," a man in a three-piece suit added. "Or you might end up in the slammer, er, calaboose."

The entire group burst into raucous laughter.

Abbey looked at the flyer to see what was causing this wild reaction on the part of the other store managers.

The flyer was the traditional mall office notice, with a candy-cane striped border around the edge, and on it red letters proclaimed: "The Candy Cane Calaboose is on its way!"

Candy Cane Calaboose? What on earth was that? She remembered seeing the construction going on down the mall corridor from her store, but she hadn't bothered to investigate further. She certainly didn't have the time to keep up with all the little "enhancements" the mall management had added this season.

Abbey shrugged, and her flyer joined the others in the recycling bin by the mailboxes. The Candy Cane Calaboose sounded like another one of the half thought-out ideas of the mall management, and certainly nothing she had the time or energy to deal with.

It was just silly, and it certainly had nothing to do with her.

Chapter 7

The pace of Christmas sales had picked up tremendously, and Abbey felt her spirits rising to meet the challenge of the increased traffic. The weather had been cooperative—except for the snowfall that had resulted in the brief skirmish she'd had with that snow bank—and the crowds in the mall had increased as Christmas approached.

The nice part about it was that she had a reason to stay at the mall from early in the morning until late at night, and when she went home she dropped into bed, exhausted, and slept. For others, that might be a nightmare, but for her, it was great. She was in her element at the store. She knew the rules, she knew the way things went, and she felt good about her abilities.

It's not the kind of life that most people dream of, she acknowledged to herself the next day as she waited for her car to warm up before leaving her house, *but it's perfect for me. Everything now is building toward a good future in business, and all the stress, all the struggle, is going to pay off, and pay off well.*

Still, a part of her argued back, *wouldn't you like to have someone to be there for you, someone to say, "Poor baby," when you complain about the shipment that didn't arrive or the salesclerk who forgets her shift? Wouldn't it be nice to have someone to talk to in the morning while your car warms up...instead of having to talk to yourself?*

She was clearly losing her mind. Sitting in her car, having a full-fledged conversation with herself about talking to herself—this was definitely not a sign of strong mental health.

She sent the wipers across the windshield in one last angry sweep. The glass wasn't entirely clear of frost, but there was a small window of visibility that she decided to take advantage of, and she backed out of the driveway.

As she crept along the road to the mall, the radio played Christmas carol after Christmas carol. She wanted to change the station, but she didn't dare take her hands off the steering wheel; she didn't want a repeat of yesterday's encounter with the snow bank.

"Joy to the World" began to play, and she recalled the hymn sing at Golden Meadows.

Golden Meadows!

She started to slap her head but remembered just in time not to let go of the steering wheel. In the bustle of the Christmas trade and the emotional chaos Mike had thrown her into, she'd forgotten to get the gift from Claire and get the mess straightened out once and for all.

For a moment, she considered writing the whole thing off as a loss, and if loopy Aunt Luellen inquired about her present, she could lie and say it had gotten lost in the mail. It was only a teeny white lie, Abbey reasoned, since Aunt Luellen had sent the gifts to the wrong address, and it was only through a momentary lapse on her part that the slippers had gotten to Claire.

Why, oh why, hadn't she simply tossed those dreadful slippers in the trash that evening?

Abbey tried to imagine how her life would have been different had she done just that. She wouldn't have met Mike's grandmother, and she probably wouldn't have gotten to know Mike better. Life would be calmer. More orderly. Peaceful.

And boring.

Mike smiled as he listened to the voice on the phone. The store was packed with people bearing lists of Christmas wishes, some carefully detailed by organized parents, others crayoned haphazardly by anxious children. Nick, his assistant, was making frantic signs at him that his help was needed with customers.

Mike waved him away, but Nick was persistent.

"Not now," Mike wrote on a piece of paper and shoved it to Nick. "In a minute."

"Who are you talking to?" his assistant asked him.

"No one," Mike mouthed at him.

"Whaaaat?"

Mike put his hand over the mouthpiece and whispered, "It's my grandmother."

"Your grandmother is not 'no one.' Honestly,

Mike, I thought more of you than that!" Nick told him indignantly.

Mike grinned. "I meant I wasn't talking. She talks. I just listen."

He returned his attention to the voice on the telephone. "Yes, Grandma," he said at last. "I'll be there. And yes, I'll do my best to do that. Yes, Grandma. I understand. Okay."

At last he hung the phone up. "I do love my grandmother," he told Nick, "but when she's got something on her mind, heaven and earth must stop until it's done."

"What's up?" Nick asked.

"The story I just heard was a long, convoluted saga about a plugged drain and a handyman shortage at Golden Meadows. I didn't follow it all, but I'll run over tonight during the supper lull and see what's up."

Any further discussion was stopped by a harried-looking woman bearing five wrinkled lists. "How does Santa do it?" she asked, juggling the packages she already carried while trying not to drop the stack of games and action toys she had picked up. "I've only got five kids, and I can't keep their lists straight."

"Volume," Mike answered. "He buys in volume."

She grinned at him. "I think that's what I'm doing today. At least, that's what my checkbook is telling me."

"Want some help? I could put those smaller packages into some larger ones with handles," he offered. "That would make them easier to carry."

"Oh, bless you. I love Christmas, even though it is a financial crunch." She heaved the packages and the toys onto the counter. "It reminds me to take another look at my children and see what miracles they are, what a fount of possibilities they are, what a gift they are. God trusted me with them—me! It humbles me every time I think about it."

"I like that," Mike commented. It was a refreshing change from the complaints he heard so often from parents who had overspent their budget to buy toys that their children wanted at the moment but might very well forget about in a week or two.

She blushed. "I know I should do this every moment of my life, but sometimes life gets in its own way, if you know what I mean. Christmas is a nudge in the side to look at those children. Okay, look at them when they're asleep, which is about the only time they're not fighting, but that's kids for you. Anyway, even with the wildest of the bunch—that'd be my Richie—I know I see the face of an angel in training."

She frowned as she looked at the pile of toys. "Could you do me a favor and add these things up? I have the dreadful feeling my Christmas Club account has run dry."

Mike totaled the items up. She sighed with relief as he told her the sum. "Just under the wire." She handed him the money. "Thank you so much for the bags— and for listening to me. Have a Merry Christmas!"

It was interesting, Mike thought as she left, how someone so unexpected could give you a gift...one you couldn't buy at any mall.

The thought of a gift reminded him that his grandmother had mentioned that Abbey hadn't picked up her gift from her aunt Luellen yet. This might be the perfect chance for her to do so. He'd stop by Trends on the way to Golden Meadows. That way

Abbey wouldn't have time to think of reasons why she shouldn't go.

For some reason, there was a special lilt in his step that carried him through the rest of the day.

Abbey put away the last of the new shipment of holiday earrings and stretched. The day had gone on endlessly. Maybe she should take a walk down the mall and get a cranberry Italian ice. It was one of the seasonal offerings the mall had that she actually liked.

"Abbey!" Mike's voiced hailed her from the front of the store. "You about ready to take a break?"

"I don't know when you started mind reading," she said, her voice only somewhat grumpy, "but I was just getting ready to go down to Italian N'Ice. Want to walk with me?"

"Sounds good, but I'm headed out to see Grandma. Would you like to join me? We can go through some hamburger joint drive-in on the way back if that's okay with you. I usually don't go for fast food, but tonight that's all I can manage—Nick is leaving early since he has a final exam at seven."

She paused, and Mike added, "Grandma isn't going to leave you alone until you go get your gift, you know. You might as well accept that. When she gets a project—and right now straightening out the confusion with the gifts is her project—she doesn't stop until it's resolved. She did mention that she has your present out there, and she suggested, as only my grandmother can suggest, that you could come out there and pick it up."

Abbey opened her mouth to object, but then

thought better of it. This might be the perfect chance for her. If they weren't going to stay long out there, she could get the package, wish Claire a Merry Christmas, and be on her way, back on track, within an hour.

It was the ideal situation.

"I'll go," she announced. The expression on his face made her add hastily, "But only to put an end to this maniac mix-up."

The evening was warmer than it had been during the day, and Mike commented on the mild temperature.

"It'll snow soon, then," Abbey said. "Didn't you pay attention to Mr. Lloyd's science class in high school, when he talked about weather?"

"He talked about weather?" Mike laughed. "Oh, that was the class that Eileen Jamison was in. No wonder I don't know anything about weather. There was no way I could concentrate on anything when she was in the room. I had such a major crush on her. Then she married some football player, like the day after graduation. My teenaged heart was broken."

"I didn't know you and Eileen were a couple," Abbey said with some surprise. Eileen had been the class president, a cheerleader, and a soloist in the chorus. Mike had always been in the background of activities.

"We were a pair in my adolescent dreams only." Mike sighed dramatically. "I don't think she even knew I was alive. Well, maybe she did. Remember that showcase that had all those dusty old trophies dating back to the turn of the century—the nineteenth century, that is?"

Abbey nodded. "I don't remember seeing it after my junior year. Didn't they finally get rid of it?"

"They had some help. I was watching Eileen in the hall one day, being the googly-eyed lovesick teenaged boy that I was, and I wasn't watching where I was going. A staircase just appeared out of nowhere, and suddenly I was going head over heels down it. As if that weren't bad enough, as I started down the stairs, I grabbed her arm—why, I don't know—and she went with me. That showcase broke our fall. Or maybe I should just say that the showcase broke."

"What did she do?" Abbey asked, laughing over the image of them tumbling down the stairs together.

"She was very polite about it. She got up, helped me up since my long gangly legs were tied into a knot, or so it seemed, and asked me if I was okay. Then she grinned and said that she had never taken that particular set of stairs so quickly or so noticeably—and that once was quite enough. So if was all right with me, she'd be taking another set of stairs for awhile—and she was doing so without my help. And that was it."

"Didn't you just about die?"

"I asked my parents to move so I could go to another school. They said no. I thought maybe I could go live on a mountaintop like those hermits but realized I would have trouble finding a mountain in this part of Minnesota. One of the troubles with being a teenager is that your range of movement is limited. So I stayed on and lived with the utter humiliation."

They discussed the trials and tribulations of being a teenager until Mike pulled into the parking lot of Golden Meadows. True to Abbey's earlier prediction, thick white flakes had begun their lazy drift from the sky. Residents were lined up at the large glass windows watching the snowfall.

It was pretty, Abbey had to admit that. The air was quiet, free from sound, and the evergreen garlands and wreath were frosted with the new snow. For this one moment, away from the bustle of the holiday mall, she could almost like Christmas.

Mike took a deep breath. He needed to talk to Abbey about the other night and apologize for his clumsiness. Hopefully he could do it without taking a header on the parking lot of Golden Meadows.

Maybe he should wait until he was inside, he told himself ruefully. He seemed to have better luck staying upright when he was inside. But he knew that once he was inside, the residents wouldn't let him have a minute alone with Abbey. Toss in the fact that the retirement home was one of Abbey's least favorite places on earth, and he realized that this wasn't the place.

He'd try the parking lot, but he just wouldn't touch her arm when he talked to her. Maybe that would help him keep his equilibrium.

It would also help if he didn't try to kiss her, he reminded himself. There was nothing wrong with being head over heels in love, but not in an icy parking lot.

Chapter 8

Mike paused a moment before entering the over-sized entrance of Golden Meadows. "I want you to know that—"

He wasn't able to finish the sentence. The door was flung open, and a crowd of elderly laughing women yelled, "Surprise!" One of them held a bough of something over his head, then stood on her tiptoes and kissed him soundly on the cheek.

"Marlys, do you have mistletoe?" he teased.

She blushed and nodded. "Yes, I do."

"Can I borrow it?" he asked with a wink.

Abbey's stomach twisted with anticipation and anxiety. Surely he wouldn't...surely he would.

Which did she want?

"Sweet's going to smooch his sugarplum," someone in the group crowed.

"That's right," he said, his eyes twinkling as he turned to look at Abbey.

Her heart and her mind waged war. She wanted him to take advantage of the mistletoe, and yet she didn't. For a moment, time held its breath.

Then he announced, his warm brown eyes twinkling, "The first kiss goes to my favorite girl."

All heads swiveled with one accord to look at Abbey. She knew she was blushing, but there wasn't a thing she could do but stand stock-still and wait for her fate.

Mike raised the mistletoe and turned to the woman who was watching from the corner. "Grandma, pucker up!"

Disappointment caught Abbey off-guard. Of all the emotions she might have expected, this was not one of them. What had she been thinking? That they'd share their first kiss in front of a group of senior citizens—when they hadn't even really dated yet?

And besides, it wasn't as if she cared about him one way or the other. He was simply a friend, a fellow retailer, and no more.

Nevertheless, the image in front of her blurred, and the carols that were piped into the great room faded into the background. She blinked her eyes rapidly and willed her emotions back into line. This was just silly. He didn't matter to her, not at all.

Mike was bent over, talking to his grandmother, an attentive expression on his face, and she was reminded that he was a good, caring man. Then he stood up and walked away.

She realized that Claire was watching her, and she forced a smile. "Claire, it's good to see you again."

Claire reached out a gnarled hand. "How nice of you to come see me! At least, I'm assuming you've come to see me."

"Of course I'm here to visit you. Shall we go to your room to visit, or is there another place you'd rather go?"

"Let's go to the Fireside Lounge and sit beside the fire. There's a big picture window there, and we can watch the snow falling. Mike will be tied up for awhile finding that reprobate handyman to unplug my drain. Can you stay?"

"Not for long. This is my dinner break."

"Have you eaten?"

"Mike and I will stop on the way back."

Claire made a face. "Not that dreadful fast food stuff, I hope."

"I'm afraid so, but just for tonight. I think we'll live through it."

The Fireside Lounge looked different than it had before. The folding chairs that had been set up for the hymn sing had been taken down, and now small tables and comfortable chairs were scattered in conversational groups throughout the room.

Abbey helped Claire settle near the fire. It was a cozy setting, with upholstered wingback chairs positioned on either side of the native-stone fireplace. A large picture window looked out on the rolling back lawn of the home, and in the starlight the pines that ringed the clearing enclosed the peaceful world.

"How are you doing, Claire?" Abbey asked, and she was amazed at how much she really did care.

"Pretty good. Oh, there are days when I'd like to complain, and maybe I do, but for the most part I'm doing well. How are things with you?" Claire's china blue eyes fixed on Abbey from behind the thick lenses of her eyeglasses.

"The store is doing well, but of course much of that right now is the Christmas trade. It'll drop off in January, after the returns are done, of course."

"Sweet says the same thing about his store." Claire leaned back contentedly. "I'd have never thought that a grown man could make a decent living selling toys, of all things, but that boy sure did prove me wrong."

"Especially this time of year," Abbey agreed. "I think everybody buys toys at Christmas."

"He's going to make a fine husband for some lucky woman," Claire said with studied casualness. "He'll be a good provider, he's not bad to look at, and he's a Christian, which counts for everything in this world."

Abbey could feel a flush rising up her neck. Had Claire seen her get flustered when Mike was fooling with the mistletoe? "He's a nice person," she said, noncommittally.

Those bright blue eyes sharpened behind the thick lenses. "He's the best, and I'm not just saying that because we're related so I have to. He really is. And it appears to me that he thinks highly of you."

Claire was clearly matchmaking. In her mind, she already had Abbey and Mike paired off, probably with 2.5 children in a house surrounded by a white picket fence and morning glories that bloomed in the morning sun. Abbey knew she had to put that idea to rest. And the best approach was the direct one.

"I'm going back to school to get my business degree," she said gently. "First my undergraduate degree in business, then my MBA. I can't do that here. I'll have to move."

Claire's lips curved a bit in a secret smile. "There are plans, and there are plans," she said enigmatically.

"My plans are real," Abbey said. "I have a ten-year strategy all worked out. I know exactly where I'll be and what I'll be doing."

Claire's smiled deepened. "The certainty of youth. Oh, I'm not going to argue with you," she said as Abbey started to interrupt. "It's always good to have a plan, but it's like the good book says: God has His own set of plans for us. Just when you think you've got it under control, God comes along and shouts, 'Surprise!' right into your heart."

"You speak like someone who's experienced that firsthand." Abbey knew that the best way to derail Claire was to change the focus of the conversation.

"God's given me many a surprise in these years He's had me on this planet. Some are good, and some…well, some weren't."

Claire paused, and Abbey watched the wave of memories wash over the elderly woman's face— twinges of pain mixed with uplifting joy.

"I've had a good life, you know—not that I'm writing the last chapter to it yet, don't get me wrong on that! But I'm happy with what the Lord has given me."

"Did you always feel that way?" Abbey asked. "I don't know how to ask this, but did you have a career outside the house?"

Claire patted Abbey's hand. "You're a dear. Yes, honey, I was a teacher until I got married and had my children, then I took some time off. I went back for awhile after they grew up and started their own lives."

"Did you have a plan?"

Mike's grandmother laughed. "A plan? I don't think they'd been invented yet! But I did have an idea of what I wanted to do and why. It's not quite the same as the life plans people do now, but it worked at the time."

Abbey stirred uncomfortably. She lived so tightly by her ten-year plan that she couldn't imagine life without it. But apparently Claire had done fine without one as detailed as hers. On the other hand, Abbey told herself, life had been simpler for Claire. Her life couldn't have been as complicated as the one Abbey led.

"We didn't have money for much of anything," Claire reminisced, "but we had lots of love. You hear that all the time, and sometimes it seems like they're just so many words. But with us it was true."

"What was your husband like?" Abbey asked.

"My Arthur was a God-fearing man—although he used to insist that he was also a Claire-fearing man. We had good times together. Lean times, sorrowful times, stressful times—they were all made better by the fact that we had each other. Abbey, don't get so caught up in your career that you overlook the importance of having someone to love—and to love you," Claire implored her with earnestness.

"I'm not overlooking that," Abbey answered stiffly. "I'll get to it when I have time. I just don't have time right now."

"Make time. Don't build walls around your heart. Your career is important, but don't let it become a prison. You have your whole life ahead of you, and I'm serious when I tell you that it's a whole lot easier when you have someone to share the burdens and the joys with."

"Claire—"

"Don't interrupt your elders, dear. I'm not through yet. Let yourself be open to love. Promise me you will."

"I will," Abbey said, but mentally she added, *In my dreams.* What Claire said had the flavor of truth, but it left a sour taste in her mouth.

"What are you ladies discussing so seriously?" Mike asked behind her.

"We're just talking about what to do with young men who sneak up and listen in on women's conversations," Claire said half-jokingly.

"I didn't hear a word," Mike said seriously, but the sparkle in his eyes made Abbey wonder if he was being completely honest. "Abbey, I don't want to hurry you, but we'd better get going."

"I'll go with you to the front," Claire said. "Mike, why don't you go ahead and start the car so it'll be at least a little bit warm for Abbey?"

Mike grinned at Abbey. "She's still trying to make me a gentleman. Okay, Grandma, I'll go." He dropped a kiss on her head. "I'll try to get over here tomorrow. Abbey, I'll pull up in front."

He left quickly, and Abbey and Claire proceeded at a more leisurely pace with Claire wheeling herself out of the room and down the corridor.

As they started down the hall back to the great room, a gentleman leaning on a cane turned toward them. "Is that Sweet's lady friend?"

Abbey recognized him from her first visit to Golden Meadows. He had been her champion when

Mike had lectured her about friendship. She looked at Claire and grinned. "Yup, she's right here, Sir. Claire's his grandmother."

He waved a hand twisted with arthritis. "That's not what I mean, and you know it, young woman. I mean you. Is that fellow treating you better or do I need to give him a piece of my mind?" He shook his cane. "I'd be glad to do it too. These young chaps have no sense of chivalry at all."

Claire grasped Abbey's arm. "Did Sweet treat you badly? What did he do?"

Laughter bubbled out of Abbey. These two darling senior citizens were ready to defend her honor, even at Mike's expense. It was utterly charming.

She leaned over and kissed Claire's furrowed forehead. "Don't worry. Mike has been a perfect gentleman."

Claire said something that sounded suspiciously like, "Rats!"

The busy evening left Mike few minutes of quiet to reflect upon the evening's events. His grandmother had called him out there on some obviously trumped-up excuse. She'd given him some line about the sink in her room being plugged up, but by the time he'd gotten ahold of the Golden Meadows handyman and they'd gone to her room, the clog had miraculously taken care of itself.

It was almost, he thought, as if she'd been maneuvering to get some time alone with Abbey. And considering how things had been going lately, that was probably exactly the reason she'd engineered the whole thing.

And there was only one reason for her to want to have time alone with Abbey.

He probably should tell her that her efforts were futile, that Abbey was the ultimate businesswoman, focused on her career only. Although, he mused, lately she had seemed to be friendlier. Perhaps his talk—no, his lecture—about friendship had gotten through to her. He still felt a bit guilty about how heavy-handed he'd been that day.

Nevertheless, she'd needed to hear every word of what he'd said. He knew what it was like to feel so tired that exhaustion swirled through your body like a living thing. He'd been there himself, and he had to admit, there were times when he still overworked himself.

But friendship was the glue that held humanity together. Abbey needed a friend, and he was willing to be that friend. Just a friend, he told himself for the thousandth time that night. That was all. A friend.

He had the same uneasy feeling he used to get when, as a child, he tried to lie to his parents.

His mind leaped back to the moment with the mistletoe. He'd truly wanted to hold it over her head, but he knew he didn't dare. Friends didn't kiss under the mistletoe, the contrary voice in his head pointed out to him. And even if he had tried, she probably would have decked him on the spot.

But hadn't he, maybe, seen hope spring into her eyes like a flash of light?

Chapter 9

"I don't have time to do it," Abbey said, staring at Mike as if he'd lost his mind. "You know perfectly well that I'm working eighty hours a week. And now you want me to do something like this? And in three days?"

He was out of his mind. That was the only reasonable explanation. He'd taken total leave of his senses. Asking her to give a presentation on career guidance, and during the busiest time of the year at Trends!

"It'd be fun," he countered. "A nice change of pace."

"Sleep would be a nice change of pace. Mike, really, I'm sure—"

"You'd reach so many lives," he interrupted. "The Jeremiah Group is a great program. We got the name from the Bible verse, Jeremiah 29:11-14."

When she didn't respond, he prompted, "The one where God says that He has plans for us."

"I'm familiar with the verse," Abbey answered, with a mental addendum: *Sort of.*

"The Jeremiah Group is made up of young women who need to hear what you have to say."

"Oh, yeah, right." She snorted. "I don't know anything special. What do I have to talk to them about?"

"A lot. They don't have guidance from the outside, so I know they'd be interested in how you decided to go into retail, and how this job you have now is a steppingstone to your career goals."

"Mike, it's Christmas. You know what that means. We never have a minute to ourselves." She motioned around the interior of Trends and realized, too late, that they were the only ones in there. "Okay, so at this particular moment no one else is here. Come back in an hour or so. Then this place will be jumping with shoppers."

He didn't say anything, and she added defensively, "It's not like I could simply show up and give a talk. I'd need time to prepare. Three days isn't enough lead time. What happened to whoever was supposed to talk to them originally?"

"She went into labor."

"Some people will do anything to get out of a commitment, won't they?" Abbey said wryly. "I'm sorry. I just can't. Not now. Maybe next spring." She turned to refolding a table display of brightly striped sweaters.

"If you don't do it, the meeting will have to be cancelled."

"So? They probably have better things to do…like

Christmas shopping." She smiled at him, but he didn't return her smile.

"Abbey," he said seriously, "these girls don't have money to shop with. That's the point of the whole thing. It's a career guidance group."

She couldn't do it, she reasoned. She kept coming back to the one irrefutable fact: She didn't have time. When would she squeeze something like this into her already overpacked day?

And besides that, she had no expertise when it came to guiding young women, especially those who were considered at risk. What would she say to them? She'd never addressed a group at all, let alone a selection of teenagers who were bound to be a reluctant and captive audience.

She knew how it would go. She'd bumble her way through, and they'd laugh at her. Maybe openly, but most certainly behind her back.

Actually, that was a best-case scenario. What if she said something terribly wrong…and messed up someone's life?

No, it was too much to ask of her. She couldn't do it.

"Plus I don't go to your church." She clutched at that straw. "I couldn't talk about religion. All I know about religion is what I got from Aunt Luellen, and loopy as she is, I wouldn't be surprised if she didn't mix up Jeremiah with Niemeier."

"Nehemiah. That doesn't matter. We'll do that part. All you have to do is come in, tell the girls a bit about how you decided what you wanted to do for a living, and talk to them about goal-setting and career-planning."

"That's all, huh?"

"Yup." He smiled at her winningly.

"How long would I have to be there?"

"An hour, hour and a half tops."

An hour? It loomed like a lifetime. She couldn't do it. She wouldn't do it. But her traitorous mouth opened, and she heard herself saying, "All right. I'll do it. Let's hope they're not expecting too much."

"You'll be great!" Mike said with enthusiasm. "I'll talk to you more about it tomorrow and see how you're doing, okay?"

"Okay." Abbey was sure she was making a monstrous mistake, but it couldn't be that bad, could it?

Mike turned at the entrance to Trends. "Oh, one more thing, Abbey."

"What's that?"

"Don't quote from the book of Niemeier."

Abbey laid out her presentation as she worked. While she was arranging a shimmering display of vests, she organized her biography. As she positioned another rack of evening gowns in an impossibly tight corner, she prepared the steps of effective goal-setting. She shifted sale purses to a table near the front of the store while she created questions sure to provoke vital and intelligent discussion.

As she drove home, she thought of the young women. She would have benefited from such a group, she knew that. Whether she would have listened when she was that age was another matter entirely. Well, all she could do was go and share what she had, and if something took root in even one girl's mind, it was a good thing.

For the first time in months, Abbey felt really good. She was energized. She was excited. She tried to ignore the fact that she was undoubtedly nuts.

Mike picked her up at Trends an hour before the Jeremiah Group was to meet. "You look nice," he commented. "I meant to tell you not to wear a suit, so what you have on is perfect."

This was the seventh outfit she'd put on. Her bed was piled with discarded dresses, slacks, and skirts. She'd finally chosen a long denim skirt and fleece vest with a turtleneck. She hoped she exuded a sense of confidence she didn't truly feel.

"Thank you," she said.

There. She was in trouble. If her voice was going to waver and wobble like that, and she hadn't even left her store, she could only imagine what a nightmare her presentation was going to be.

Mike put his hand on her arm. "Abbey, these are girls who are starting from ground zero. Some of them may even be below that. Don't be afraid of them."

"I'm not afraid of them," she said defensively, lifting her chin just a bit. "What I'm scared of is myself. What if I blow it?"

"You'll be fine."

"I hope you're right." Abbey's hands were sweating as she pulled on her yellow mittens. Their bright wool reflected a cheerfulness she didn't feel.

Mike talked about everything except the presentation as they drove to his church, Word of Faith Community Church. She'd seen it before, but she'd never gone in. It was a simple pale brown brick building with a white-painted steeple and cross.

Every muscle in her body urged her to turn back as she and Mike entered the building. But the window of opportunity closed quickly, and she was soon enveloped with warm greetings of others who were waiting inside.

"It's so nice of you to do this," one woman said. "I have everything ready for you, even a laptop and a projector."

The woman took Abbey's coat and introduced herself as Mrs. Robbins. "I'm one of the counselors for the Jeremiah Group," she explained. "There are many people involved with the program. Mike, for example, coordinates the speakers. My specialty is helping the young women with filling out job applications and going to interviews."

"It sounds interesting," Abbey commented, realizing it was a bland statement that didn't really focus in on what Mrs. Robbins was saying.

"The girls in this group—and they are rather young this time—need this kind of assistance. Whatever we can offer them is beneficial. In some cases, their parents don't work, or they rely on seasonal or part-time employment. Two of them have been shuttled around in foster homes so much that they don't have a clear picture of what a career even is. That's why what you're saying to them today is so important."

Mrs. Robbins motioned to a nearby room. A green-and-gold plaid curtain hid the interior from view, but from the way the drape moved a bit, Abbey knew she was being observed. She was only faintly aware of the curious gazes studying her covertly. She was using all her energies to keep from passing out from stage fright.

Mrs. Robbins saw Abbey's glance and smiled. "They'll be very distant, almost detached, but don't let that bother you. That's their defense against a world that often makes them into outsiders. Being aloof is their way of turning the tables."

Abbey could understand that. She had been through a rebellious stage herself, although what she'd been rebelling against was still a mystery to her. It was probably just teenaged angst.

"Shall we go in?" Mrs. Robbins asked, leading her toward the curtained room. Abbey was sure that mortal embarrassment waited for her.

They had done all that they could to fill the requests she made and to make her feel welcome, and with fearful feet she went in to meet the Jeremiah Group.

A flurry of activity greeted their entrance as the young women scurried away from the window that looked out on the narthex. They made a great show of not being at all interested in the guest as they gathered in the far corner and talked lazily to each other.

"Don't let them deter you," Mrs. Robbins whispered. "They're dying to meet you."

I'm the one who's dying, Abbey thought. This was the modern day equivalent of being thrown to the lions. Didn't that happen in the Bible? She remembered seeing a vivid picture in her children's Bible of a man sitting amidst a group of ferocious lions.

Scrap that. Insert a picture of a completely terrified

store manager surrounded by a small group of bored young women. Truly a horrific scenario.

She looked at her tormentors. There were fourteen of them in attendance that day, most of them in their mid to late teens. Some viewed her with hostility, some with smiles, some with suspicion.

Her mouth was suddenly very dry, and the first words she had formulated to speak wouldn't come out at all. The teens watched her with increasing interest, inquisitiveness edging into their expressions as she continued to stand in front of them, mute.

It was just as she had feared. It was like one of those dreams she used to have in which she was addressing Congress in her pajamas, the fuzzy white ones with the chickens printed in bright yellow. The women's faces faded in and out again, and for a moment she thought she was going to be sick. That might not be such a bad thing, she reflected, because then she could leave.

She turned pleadingly at last to Mike. He'd have to take over and save her.

Sure enough, Mike stepped into the breach. He introduced her, then said, "Let's open in prayer. Blessed Father, guide Abbey's words as she speaks to the members of this group. Guide our ears that we might learn from her. And guide our feet as we go forth with today's message. Amen."

Abbey shot him a look of surprise. "That was short," she whispered.

"Cool, huh?" Mike grinned at her and turned his attention back to the assemblage. One woman chewed on the edge of her fingernail while another curled a lock of her hair around her finger. They could not have looked less interested.

Yet Mike persisted. "You all know that this group got its name from Jeremiah 29:11-14, right? God has plans for you, but there's absolutely nothing wrong with helping Him along and making the most of the talents He gave you. That's what Abbey is here to talk to you about—maximizing your time and your talents. Let's welcome her."

Some lackluster applause accompanied Abbey as she faced the group again. She knew her first instincts had been right. She shouldn't be here. What on earth had she been thinking of? What kind of insanity had overtaken her when she agreed to do it?

I need some help here. If there was ever a good time for prayer, this was it.

The sea of faces swam into focus. One by one, she looked directly at each young woman and saw them as individuals, not a homogenous group of blasé girls. Their eyes met hers, and in that moment of contact, each teenager let Abbey see past the artifice. She saw the fear of rejection behind the bravado, the hurt behind the mask of boredom.

The words she had so carefully prepared vanished from her mind, and suddenly they were replaced by words from her heart. The group quit shifting in their seats and focused their attention on her. The young women watched her, transfixed, and her speech gained power. She talked about finding her talent and making the most of it, and the satisfaction of knowing that she was doing what she was meant to do, and doing it well.

The teenagers rarely looked away as she talked.

And finally, she realized she was through. Her energy reservoirs were totally depleted, and she felt as limp as cooked spaghetti.

Mike stood and shook her hand. "That was wonderful. Thank you so much for coming today and sharing your expertise with us. Abbey will stay for a few minutes if you want to talk to her some more. I'm sure she won't mind answering any extra questions you might have."

There was a moment of silence before the worldly cloaks fell back over their eyes and they retreated to their facade of coolness. Yet as soon as Mike left the podium and the session was clearly over, in one wave of movement, the young women stood and came forward to surround Abbey.

Mike sighed with relief. Abbey had done extremely well to get this kind of reaction from them. He offered up a quick prayer of thanksgiving for the success of her talk. Not only did the girls need it, he sensed, but Abbey did too.

Finally the last teenager drifted away, and Mike moved over to where she was standing. "You must have been quite the success," he said. "These girls may be anywhere from fourteen to eighteen in chronological age, but in street years, they're much older. They're usually so blasé that we're lucky they're not doing their nails during the presentation. And you were worried!"

To his amazement, she sat down and put her head in her hands.

"What's the matter?" he asked.

"Are you ready for this? They all had the same

question." Abbey shook her head in amazement, but she didn't look up.

"Really? What was it? Did they want details on how to find career counseling or something like that?"

"No." Her shoulders began to shake.

Mike ran his fingers through his hair. Why was she crying? He never knew what to do when adults cried.

"Did they have educational concerns, like where to find a school?"

"Not exactly."

"They were intrigued by a career in retail?"

"Um, sort of," she hedged. She raised her eyes, and he realized that she had not been crying. She was laughing. "They wanted to know where I got my vest."

They looked at each other, and together they howled with laughter. It was getting to be a habit with them, this roaring into uncontrollable laughter over the most inane things. But it was a nice habit.

"It's so absurd," Abbey said at last. "All of that emotion, that worry, that preparation, and all they wanted to know is where I got my stupid vest."

"It's good advertising for Trends," Mike said.

"No, it isn't." Abbey couldn't avoid the absurdity of the situation. "I got it at the discount store at the other mall about four years ago. I had no idea what to tell them, so I just said I'd had it for ages."

"Do you feel bad that you put so much work into the presentation only to have it turn out this way?" Mike asked gently.

It was a legitimate question, and Abbey's response was a bit surprising to her. "I've got to admit it would have been a lot simpler if I could have had them come over to my house and go through my closet, if that's what you mean. But yes, it's a bit distressing. All that planning, only to find out I'd been preparing for the wrong thing. Go figure."

"You know," Mike said, standing and reaching for their coats, "the verse in Jeremiah applies to you too. We don't know what God's plans are for us. We can only trust that He won't do anything too rash to set things in motion. Maybe one of these teenagers has had her life changed today by that woman in the dynamite vest. It could be that's why you wore it today."

She remembered the many changes of clothes before she'd decided on this particular outfit, how often she'd tossed aside an outfit simply because it didn't "feel right." Could he be onto something? She'd heard that there were no true accidents.

Mike continued as they left the little church, "And who knows, you may very well have touched someone's heart here today in a way you can't know."

She'd touched a heart, all right, he acknowledged, *but God, did it have to be mine?*

Chapter 10

Abbey was still chuckling over the incident the next day. She was telling Selma about it when suddenly a man dressed in a Keystone Kops outfit, complete with a rounded helmet and a billy club, invaded her store.

"Officer Oliver P. Torkelson here. I have a warrant for Abbey Jensen," he said loudly. "I've come to arrest you!" His handlebar moustache tilted forward dangerously, and he shoved it back into place.

"What on earth?" Abbey asked. She'd never seen anything like this. "You must have the wrong place, or at least the wrong person."

"You're under arrest, young lady. The charge is— wait a second, let me check." He pulled a folded sheet of paper from his shirt pocket with great ceremony and proceeded to read: "Abbey Jensen is hereby placed under arrest for being a Holiday Hooligan."

"A Holiday Hooligan? What is that? This is crazy!"

"Got the warrant right here. All written out proper-like. You'd better come with me."

"I'm not coming with you," Abbey protested. "I have no idea what this is all about."

"Sorry, Ma'am." Torkelson produced gigantic red plastic handcuffs. "Resisting arrest means I'll have to use these."

A strangled sound from behind her made Abbey turn her head. Selma was overcome with giggles. "Do you know anything about this?" Abbey asked her employee warily. "You do, don't you?"

Selma shook her head wordlessly.

"Mike. Mike had something to do with it," Abbey accused. "And from that grin on your face, you do too know what's going on."

Officer Torkelson cleared his throat loudly. "Enough chitchat. You'd better come with me to the Candy Cane Calaboose."

"The Candy Cane Calaboose?" Abbey repeated. "What is that?"

The policeman tsked and wrote something on the warrant. "I'm going to have to add Failure to Read Merry Mall Mail to the complaint."

"Merry Mall Mail?" Abbey couldn't believe her ears. "I've never heard of such a thing."

"That's because you never read your Merry Mall Mail," Officer Torkelson said logically. "If you'd have read it, you'd know what it was."

Abbey covered her face with her hands. "This is unreal. I never heard of Merry Mall Mail. I don't know what the Candy Cane Calabash is."

"Calaboose," Selma corrected. "A calaboose is a jail. A calabash is a gourd."

"Calabash, calaboose. This is insane."

Officer Torkelson stroked his moustache reflectively. "Trying to cop an insanity plea, eh? Are you insane? Do I need to get a straightjacket?"

"No, I'm not insane. They're insane, whoever 'they' are. And I certainly don't need a straightjacket." She paused as she realized what was transpiring. "Oh, for crying out loud. This is what the other managers were talking about down at the mailboxes, isn't it? Please tell me this isn't the brainchild of the mall management."

The policeman's moustache twitched dangerously.

She knew she had no choice except to go. Selma would watch the store, and besides, it would probably be just a few minutes. Even the mall administration wouldn't be as silly as to take people off the selling floor during the busiest season of the year for any extended period of time.

"This won't take long," she told Selma grimly as she left in the custody of Officer Torkelson. "And if it gets busy, call the mall office. This is their idea, so they might as well reap the results of it."

She'd walked by the Candy Cane Calaboose, but she hadn't paid much attention to it other than to note that it was another way of making use of every inch of the mall's space. The wooden structure was clearly modeled after an old-fashioned jail but with one crucial exception: the bars on the cells were painted in red and white spirals.

"Here, put this on." A woman dressed in a skirt

and blouse printed with tiny candy canes handed her a bundle. "These are your jail coveralls."

Abbey shook them out. They were striped, like the prisoner outfits of the old movies, but instead of black and white, these were red and white, like candy canes.

"I can't put these on," Abbey objected. "I'm wearing a skirt, in case you hadn't noticed."

"Just pull them on top," the woman instructed her. "By the way, I'm the warden here, so don't get snippy with me." She shook the large key that hung around her neck, which was apparently used with the oversized heart-shaped lock on the cell door. The twinkle in her eyes softened her words, and she added in a whisper, "It could have been a lot worse. They started out with this being a dunking tank, so count your blessings."

Abbey shuddered at the thought of what havoc that idea would have wrought. "The mall management has had some nutso ideas," she muttered as she pulled the coveralls over her clothes, "but this takes the cake."

Her skirt bunched up around her hips under the coverall, and she was sure she looked as if she had the world's biggest caboose. The Candy Cane Caboose, she told herself.

"Did you see that you have company?" the woman added, pointing to a second chair in the cell.

Abbey had almost missed him, but how, she couldn't have said. Mike was also garbed in the candy-striped coverall.

"You look ridiculous," she said, plopping into the vacant chair. "Kind of like an oversized after-dinner mint."

"They don't call me Sweet for nothing," he quipped.

"Fill me in on this, please," she said. "Apparently I didn't read my Merry Mall Mail—whatever that is—but I have no idea who ratted on me. And I was certainly never aware that it was an offense that was going to get me arrested."

He chuckled. "Here's the scoop. Anybody at the mall—employees, customers, competitors, whatever—can pay to have you put in the slammer, er, calaboose. And there you stay until someone bails you out. All the money goes to charity."

"A noble goal," she grumbled. "So what you're saying is that somebody, some rat fink, paid to have me put here?" She glowered at him suspiciously.

"First of all, I don't believe I've heard someone actually say 'rat fink' in the past decade, and secondly, don't glare at me. I thought you were responsible for me being here, but since you are clueless about this whole Candy Cane Calaboose thing, I guess I have to blame one of my employees."

She recalled Selma's bout with hysterics when Abbey was "arrested." "I think I know who the culprit is...at least for me being stuck in here. Selma."

A sudden thought struck her. Selma was a one-person fan club for romance; it wouldn't be too hard to imagine her putting both Abbey and Mike in the Candy Cane Calaboose at the same time.

Mike leaned back and hummed along with the public address system, which boomed non-stop Christmas carols at top volume. Abbey craned her neck and noticed that they were positioned directly under a circular speaker embedded in the wall.

"I used to love those songs," she mused. "But somewhere around November tenth, they lost their appeal."

"You're kidding!" Mike seemed genuinely surprised. "I love the whole Christmas scene. Carols, trees, presents, the whole nine yards."

Abbey motioned at the mall outside their cell. "But look at this. 'Gaudy' doesn't even begin to describe it. They've added another scene. A purple plaster seal wearing a wreath around its neck. Isn't that charming?"

"The seal is inexplicable. I don't know what that's doing here." Mike cocked his head and studied the statue. "No, I can't say as I see any reason for it to be here. It's ludicrous at best."

"Well, that's my point. What does it have to do with Christmas?"

He leaned forward earnestly. "That isn't Christmas. That's profit margins, pure and simple—if there is anything pure or simple about profit margins. The seal has more to do with the mall manager and his exquisite artistic taste than the future of a major world religion. Christmas is about the birth of hope. It's the first day of our salvation."

"You sound like my aunt Luellen." The conversation made Abbey uneasy, but at the same time she craved talking about her confused feelings. And oddly, having this discussion about Jesus in the midst of this crazy Candy Cane Calaboose made it easier.

"Your aunt Luellen is pretty smart."

"My aunt Luellen is a kook. She's the reason we're even having this talk. If it weren't for her getting those packages mixed up, we'd still be going on with our lives…separately. And I wouldn't even be thinking about Jesus or God or anything except my own profit margins."

"Like I said," Mike said, so softly she had to crane to hear his words, "your aunt Luellen is a very smart person."

Abbey snorted in derision. "How can you say that? That would mean that Aunt Luellen would have done this…on purpose," she ended slowly as the realization of what he was saying dawned on her.

There comes a moment in love when time stands still—or wishes it could. And just as frequently, that instant is pushed away in the flurry of life.

She liked him, she told herself. That was all. He was a nice guy. Okay, he was a nice guy with very nice eyes and a very nice smile and a very nice way of approaching life. But she didn't love him. Love meant—well, she couldn't define it, not here in a makeshift jail in the midst of a busy mall filled with curious shoppers. She'd have to think about it. But the fact was that she was pretty sure she'd know if she was in love. At least there would be—or should be—fireworks and volcanoes and shooting stars. She didn't feel any of that when she saw Mike. What she felt was a pleasant warmth, like the good basic meal they had at Ginger's the other night. Nothing fancy. Plain home cooking didn't equal love.

The food analogy made her hungry.

She looked at him covertly. He was a bit pinker than usual. Was it possible? Was Mike Tucker blushing? Or was it only the reflection of his candy-striped jail coveralls?

She had to change the subject, and fast. "I wonder

if they feed us in this Candy Cane Calaboose," she said. "I'm starving."

Mike seemed as equally grateful for the switch in the direction their conversation was taking. "Even a candy cane would be welcome. I think that woman who's supposed to be our warden probably has some. Want me to get one for you?"

Abbey shook her head. "I don't know if I'll ever be able to look a candy cane in the eye again."

Mike hooted with laughter. "I didn't know candy canes had eyes, but I get your point."

"How can you be so cheerful about this shenanigan?" she asked crossly, but before he could answer, a voice hailed them from the mall corridor.

"Yoo-hoo, Candy Cane captives!" Selma was approaching them, and obviously enjoying their predicament entirely too much. "Ready to get out?" She waved a ten-dollar bill at them.

"Am I ever!" Abbey stood up. "Pay my bail, and let's go. Say, if you're here, who's watching the store?"

"I closed it."

"You what?" Abbey thundered.

"Oh, I'm just kidding. Brianna came in." Selma walked around and studied the jail from the outside. "This isn't too bad. I've lived in worse places."

Mike grinned. "It's about the size of my apartment, now that you mention it. Are you springing both of us, or just Abbey?"

"Both of you. You two ready to go?"

As Abbey sprang to her feet, Mike touched her arm. "It hasn't been that bad, has it?"

The sharp retort that sprang to her lips died, and the truth—in a single word—replaced it. "No."

* * *

That evening, as Mike said his nightly prayers, he asked for reassurance. It wasn't something he often did, usually choosing instead to trust in his Father's leadership.

I'm trying, Lord. Every time I think I've taken a step closer, though, she steps back. This would be a lot easier if she'd just stay still. Am I doing this right? And, by the way, God, am I supposed to be falling in love with her?

And across town, a young woman found herself in an unusual position, her head bent and her heart open. "Tell me what to do about the way I feel," she said quietly, although who she was speaking to, she couldn't have said.

Chapter 11

Abbey leaped out of bed, horrified at the bright light that shone in through her window. Clearly she had overslept. A quick glance at the clock beside her bed verified it. It was nearly eight. She pulled back the curtain and peeked outside. Already the first round of rush hour was underway, with the late-to-work drivers stretching the speed limit.

Usually she was up early, quick to get ready for her busy day and always the first one at the mall. What was happening to her? She hadn't overslept in a couple of years. Crazy dreams had haunted her sleep, dreams filled with dancing candy canes and prisons made of sweets.

And Mike. He'd been in all of her dreams, all night long.

Once when she was in high school, studying French, her teacher had told her that when she dreamed in French, she could be assured that she had total command of the language, that she totally understood it. What did that mean when she dreamed about Mike?

She'd never dreamed in French anyway, she told herself as she slurped down a gulp of too-hot coffee, so she'd never had the chance to test the hypothesis. She needed to wake up and quit worrying about such inane stuff.

Customers were already browsing through the sales racks as she slipped into her spot behind the cash register at Trends.

Selma glanced at her curiously. "Oversleep?"

Abbey nodded. "I couldn't believe it myself." She busied herself with rearranging the display of glittery necklaces and earrings. "I guess there's something about winter that makes me want to hibernate."

Her associate snorted inelegantly. "There's something about working sixteen-hour days that makes you want to hibernate." Selma put her hand over Abbey's and stilled her active fingers. "Quit dinking around with that stuff and look at me. You need to take a break. You're working too hard and too long—"

"It's Christmas," Abbey replied, as if that explained it all.

"So go have a Christmas. Even a couple of hours. Go shopping. Drive around and look at the lights. Sit at home and watch that Christmas special with Charlie Brown and Snoopy."

As Selma spoke, Abbey felt a hunger rise in her, almost palpably. She wanted to shop, to look at lights, to watch Charlie Brown with his pitiful little tree.

She nodded. "I will. I promise. Tonight I'll take a break."

Selma looked at her with unsure eyes. "You'd better. A promise is a promise, and I'm holding you to it. You're missing the best part of Christmas, hanging out inside this mall day in and day out."

"Okay, okay, you've made your point!" Abbey cried with exasperation. "I'll do it, I promise!"

"It's four o'clock," Selma said pointedly when the afternoon rush had tapered off.

"I know. Did you want a break?" Abbey began sizing the sale blouses.

"Yes, I do, but not for me. For you. You promised."

"And I will." Abbey stooped to pick up a blouse whose hanger had broken. "Selma, can you get another hanger for this?"

"I'm going to keep after you until you go," Selma warned. "Brianna will be here in less than an hour, and then you have no excuses, M'lady."

"But who—"

"I don't know because I'm not going to listen to your question so I can't answer it. But you are going to go. How do I know? Because I can be the world's biggest pain in the neck when I need to."

Abbey grumbled under her breath.

"I heard that," Selma snapped. "I'm not sure what you said, but I can't think it was nice. Now go."

"All right." Abbey gave in grudgingly. "But first I'm off to grab a bite to eat. I'm just running down to that pretzel place, then I'll be back to do those markdowns."

Selma barred her way. "You will not. You promised me you were going to take the evening off, and I'm holding you to it. Brianna will be in to cover tonight, and there's that high school student backing her up. The store will be fine tonight. Go get some R & R."

Abbey couldn't summon the strength to argue. "You win. I'll be back tomorrow morning."

"Good. Now, at the very least, I want you to promise me you'll get in your jammies with some popcorn and veg out in front of the tube. Either the Peanuts special or *It's a Wonderful Life*." Selma almost pushed her into her coat.

"They might not be on tonight," Abbey protested lightly.

"Ha. It's December. They'll be on." Selma's laughter followed Abbey as she left the store.

Mike smiled as he stopped at the door to Trends. He'd come to see if Abbey wanted to go back to Golden Meadows, but Selma's voice had stopped him. He was glad he hadn't barged on in.

Abbey didn't even see him as she swept out with her coat on. That was good. She needed to get away for awhile, and it didn't matter where she was going: home, grocery store, Laundromat. Just as long as she wasn't living her life here in the mall.

He'd seen the little lines that were beginning to etch themselves around her eyes. She was far too young for that hard-worn look. Exhaustion radiated from her like an aura. Abbey clearly needed someone to make her leave the mall once in awhile, someone to insist that she take some time to herself.

That's why he wanted her to go with him to Golden

Meadows. That's why he was going to ask her to go to dinner with him tomorrow night. She was a child of the heavenly Father, and she deserved time to relax. That's why he was taking her away.

And it had nothing, nothing at all to do with the way her gray eyes made him feel suddenly warm and protective.

Her car sputtered and bucked. Abbey's eyes darted to the dial on the dashboard. Gas. She'd forgotten gas.

Luckily the station by the mall was open, and she basically coasted into the bay.

"Fill 'er up?" the attendant asked.

"Oh, no, I can—" she stammered in confusion. Then she realized she had driven into the full-service bay. A slow smile crossed her face. "No, go ahead. Fill it up."

It felt nice to let someone do this simple task for her. She leaned against the headrest and felt the tension try to leave her body. And she felt the resistance of habit. Go. Do. Get busy.

They were hard habits to let go of.

"Don't forget to plug in tonight."

The voice of the station attendant startled her. "What?"

"Plug in tonight. Supposed to be eighteen below." He clasped his hands together and rubbed them briskly. "Already twelve below."

She thanked him for the reminder. Minnesota winter evenings were sometimes so cold that cars needed block heaters so they'd start in the morning. Born and bred Minnesotan, Abbey thought briefly that any car without the plug hanging out of the front grillwork looked odd.

She paid for her gas and headed home. Popcorn and a television movie did sound heavenly. If she tried really hard, she might be able to get into this relaxing stuff.

But success isn't measured by how much you're relaxed, a nasty little voice whined inside her head. *It's measured by how much you've achieved, and you're not going to achieve anything by lolling around the house.*

One night, she told herself, *just this one night.* It was an experiment to see what it was like.

The wind whistled around her ears as she dug the plug-in out of the snow bank. The fellow at the gas station was right: it was already cold enough tonight to plug in her car. She hurried through the task and was glad to get inside to the warmth of her small house.

One of these days she'd actually do something to decorate the inside. The house was still painted the same bland off-white it had been when she'd bought it. The furniture was, to put it bluntly, practical, and that was all. It was the same couch, chair, bed, and table that she'd had when she was in college.

But before she committed herself to anything, she would think about what kind of furniture she wanted. And that took time. She didn't have time.

She shed her suit and wrapped a thick terry-cloth robe around her. Popcorn, then the television.

Abbey pulled open first one cabinet, then another. They seemed to gape at her. Where was the popcorn? Didn't she just buy some? She shook her head as she realized that she had last bought popcorn nearly a year ago.

"Okay, no popcorn." She shut the last cabinet door, perhaps a little harder than necessary, and opened the freezer. It was well-stocked with frozen dinners. "And this, my friends," she intoned to an imaginary group of visitors, "is what the larder of the busy career woman is like. Cabinets are empty while the freezer is stocked."

She'd make a list, she decided, and put everything she needed on it. She returned to the bare cupboard shelves. It was amazing how empty, how totally empty her shelves were.

"Okay," she continued aloud, "first item: everything."

She microwaved a macaroni and cheese dinner, figuring that was as close to popcorn as she was going to get, and sat down in front of the television with the remote control.

Click.

The screen lit up with fuzzy static. She tried another channel. It was no better. And on through all the channels, still no picture.

"Stupid cable company," she muttered, getting up to shuffle to the phone and call them.

Abbey punched in the numbers with a vengeance. "Hello, this is Abbey Jensen. My cable isn't working."

She gave them the pertinent information, then paused, aghast, at what she heard. "I haven't had cable since when? No, I guess I haven't turned on my television since then. Oh, no, no need to come out. No, I don't want the service started again. Thanks, though."

She hung up the phone and stood motionless, staring at the mute television screen.

She hadn't had cable in five months. She'd been disconnected when she hadn't responded to a switch in service. And she'd never realized it.

Abbey sank to the kitchen chair beside her. She didn't know she was out of popcorn, and she didn't even know she didn't have cable TV. Could it be worse?

How had her life gotten so far away from her? No wonder she spent so much time at Trends. She didn't have a life at all.

That wasn't true, she argued with herself. She had a VCR, and she could rent a movie and watch it. The more she thought about it, the better the idea sounded. There was a video store just around the corner. Actually, she could even walk there.

She quickly changed from her robe to a pair of woolen pants and her thickest sweater and piled on a coat, boots, mittens, and hat. She stuck her VideoVideo card in her pocket and headed out.

The crisp air froze the inside of her nostrils. That, she told herself as she strode enthusiastically through the December night, was one of the best things about living in the north. Where else could you experience that?

The cloudless sky sparkled with a few random stars that were powerful enough to overcome the lights of the city. Abbey stood still and tried to pick out Orion's belt and the Big Dipper.

A sudden memory shot into her mind, like a long-forgotten message. She had been tiny, two or three perhaps, and on such a winter night as this, her parents had bundled her up and driven her out of town, far away from the streetlamps and house lights, to the absolute darkness of the countryside where her father pulled the car over.

Abbey could still remember the rush of cold air invading the heated car as they took her out. And there, as her mother held her, still wrapped in too many layers of quilts, her father pointed out the constellations in a sky that seemed to have too many stars.

"This is Cassiopeia. See her throne? Orion the Hunter: that's his belt, those three stars in a row. The Pleiades, the Seven Sisters. The North Star is at the end of the Big Dipper's handle. Sailors used it to navigate by, and it's still the first star our eyes see in the heavens."

On and on he talked, naming the magical constellations, most of which her young eyes could not take in, but even now she remembered her mother's warm breath on her cold cheek and her father's calming voice. She was cocooned in their love.

She missed them.

A tear threatened to slide down her face but began to freeze. Abbey swiped at it with her gloved hand. There was no time for this foolishness. And it would never do to step into VideoVideo teary.

The video rental store was so bright her eyes hurt after being in the dark night. A teenager, so tall and thin that his long-sleeved VideoVideo shirt could cover only part of his arms, approached her. "Can I help you find something?"

Abbey sniffled. The problem with that marvelous

feeling of breathing in icy air is that when she got into a warm room, her nose began to run. "Yes. I'm looking for *It's a Wonderful Life*."

"Right here." The boy stretched one long arm and snagged a video from the Christmas display at the register. "Can I see your card?"

She pulled the card from her pocket and handed it to him. The clerk frowned. "This expired three years ago."

"You're kidding me!" Abbey snatched it from his hand with more gusto than she intended. "How can that be? Why, I just—" She sighed. It had been that long. "Fine. I'll get a new one."

"Okay. I need a picture ID." The teenager handed her a clipboard with a pencil dangling from a grimy string.

"ID?" she asked blankly. "I don't have my ID with me. Can't you just reactivate my old card?"

"Not after three years. Sorry, but it's—"

"Company policy," she finished for him. "I know, I know."

"You know, you could buy it for only $4 more. There's a special right now, it being Christmas and all."

"Oh, I don't need to—" she began, then stopped. *Four dollars,* she told herself. *Four dollars. Bend, Abbey. Bend and breathe.*

"That sounds like a deal," she said brightly.

What's wrong with me? she asked herself as she hurried home, the video tucked under arm. She'd forgotten the present at Golden Meadows, she'd neglected to put gas in her car, she was out of popcorn and just about everything else to eat, her cable TV bill wasn't paid, and now her video card had expired.

What else could happen?

She stared at the VCR. A tangle of cords emerged from the back of it, and somehow they were supposed to be hooked up to her television and who knew what else. Abbey sank to the floor and put her head in her hands as she remembered. She'd bought it, and as she was trying to put it together, she had been called back to Trends.

And she'd never gotten back to finishing it.

Well, she told herself, *it can't be brain surgery.* She bravely took a cord and studied the back of the television. There was no place that it fit. She checked the other end of the cord. Nope.

If she had the directions, she could figure this out. But she had no idea where they might be.

Call Mike. She knew she could do that. He undoubtedly knew how to put one of these monstrosities together, just like he probably put gas in his car, paid his bills, stocked his cupboards, and never let his memberships lapse.

Or, she told herself, she could do it herself. Not that she had any idea how to do it, but she could certainly sit down and give it a shot.

Surrounded by mysterious wires and cords, the VCR on her lap and her television turned out so that the back faced the living room, she put it together. It would have been easier with the directions, but it was possible.

Soon, *It's a Wonderful Life*—her own copy—was playing as she curled on the couch, snuggly wrapped in pajamas and robe, a bowl of freshly popped pop-corn—purchased at the video store—in her lap. But Abbey was completely unaware of George Bailey's plight.

She was sound asleep, snoring lightly, with the remnants of a satisfied smile on her face.

Chapter 12

Abbey awoke from her exhausted sleep with the instinctive feeling something was wrong. Had she overslept again? She'd been doing that a lot lately, it seemed, even if only for fifteen minutes. She had her morning regime down perfectly, and the slightest variation threw her off. She glanced at the alarm clock.

It was still early. The alarm wasn't set to go off for another half hour.

She knew she couldn't go back to sleep, but she didn't want to get up. It was too cold. The only reason it would be this cold was because the power was out, and the way the window shook told her why.

Blizzard.

She sighed and resisted the urge to tunnel deeper into the covers. Instead, she threw back the blankets and shivered as her feet touched the frigid floor. She pulled her thick robe on and tied it tightly, a faint defense against the chilly bedroom.

The hall, usually brightly sunlit, was shrouded in grayish white, the color reserved for an intense snowstorm. Abbey padded into the living room and peered at the thermostat. Sixty-four degrees. Not bad. There had been days in August when sixty-four degrees would have seemed like a blessing, she reminded herself.

A gust of wind made the windows chatter in their frames. This was a major blizzard indeed. It must have just started, because the wind was picking up speed even as she listened.

She was a good Minnesotan. She knew what to do. The first thing was to determine if it was just her house that was suffering from the power outage, or if it was everyone. She crossed to the window and drew back the curtain.

The houses on her street could have been lit up like Las Vegas, and she wouldn't have been able to tell, the storm was that intense. She couldn't see anything except a wall of white.

White-out. She hated this part of winter storms, when she couldn't see more than an inch or two in front of her face.

As if angry, the wind rattled the panes of glass even more. White snow, once so fluffy and Christmassy, had become suddenly granular and menacing. She couldn't see past the curtain of white that blew sideways, obscuring even her car.

Almost idly she thought that she should have put it in the garage last night. Now she'd have to dig it out.

Then Abbey laughed out loud. At the rate this storm was raging, she'd be shoveling one way or the other.

One thing was clear: She couldn't tell if it was just her house or if the entire block was powerless. She checked the phone. It was dead too.

What she needed now was light and some way to make coffee. She rummaged through her closet until she found what she was looking for. It was a centerpiece she'd gotten as a housewarming gift—from Aunt Luellen, now that she thought about it—and had never used. In the midst of a fuchsia raffia circle studded with oversized fake roses was a huge glaringly pink monstrosity of a candle, with three wicks and a definite strawberry scent. Right now it seemed lovely.

Abbey had a plan. All she had to do was find something to light the thing with, and she'd be in business.

She dug in the utensil drawer fruitlessly until she had an idea. Bracing herself against the cold, she zipped into the garage, grabbed the barbecue lighter off the hook on the wall, and tore back inside.

Abbey clicked it, and a flame sprang into life. She felt ridiculously happy to see it.

"And now, my strawberry-pink eyesore, you are about to make yourself useful."

She spent the next few minutes rigging up a metal measuring cup and a coat hanger. She did some quick pouring, measuring, and stirring, and after waiting somewhat patiently, was rewarded with a warmish cup of coffee. It was not Starbucks by any means, but she said to herself as she cradled the precious cup in her hands, it was coffee.

The next matter of business was getting warm.

She had a fireplace, but she hadn't gotten around to getting firewood. Her only option was to put on more clothes. Abbey pulled on another sweatshirt and wrapped the throw from the couch around her shoulders.

The batteries in her transistor radio were dead, so she shook one out of her alarm clock and commandeered another from the miniature flashlight the bank had given her and finally tuned in a local radio station. The reception was uneven at best. Static cut through the announcer's words, but she hung on every syllable.

"Lines are down...neighborhoods south of...plows are waiting out the storm..."

The sporadic news was her link with the outside world. There was nothing quite like being in a blizzard to make a person feel isolated. The swirling snow shut out everyone and everything.

"...Senior citizens...residents are urged to use caution...hypothermia...and small children...."

Claire. She hoped Claire was all right. Certainly Golden Meadows had a back-up plan—at least a better plan than she had. She grimaced at the gaudy pink candle and the rig she'd designed to make coffee. She was pitiful.

Anyone would have a better severe weather plan than she had. Mike, for example, was the kind who'd have flashlights with batteries. She didn't even know where hers was, and if she did find it, she was sure the batteries would be too old. No, she had to rely on a grotesquely pink candle for her light and heat.

Actually, knowing Mike, he probably had all the

residents of his apartment building gathered in one room, singing "Kumbaya."

That was mean-spirited, she knew. It was just that she had let everything slide. Everything, except her career. That she had firmly in her grip. She needed to take comfort from that.

"Closed... Also the schools, the mall, the post..."

That was what she was listening for. The mall was closed.

Mike pulled the drapes shut on the window of his apartment. He'd seen enough. This wasn't going to be one of those blizzards that blew through quickly. No, this blizzard was settling in for awhile.

It was hard to concentrate when the walls of the apartment shook with every windy blast. That was one of the problems of living on the fourth floor. It seemed as if his floor took the brunt of the storms.

If the electricity were on, he could watch television, or maybe a videotaped movie. He told himself he could read a book, but the fact was he didn't want to. He couldn't concentrate on it.

He was glad he'd chosen this apartment. It had a fireplace, so he was warm. But despite the comfort of the fireplace, he couldn't shake a feeling of worry. He knew that his grandmother would be safe at Golden Meadows. The generator would keep the heating system going, and there were round-the-clock aides to reassure the residents. But he wished the phones were working so he could call Abbey. Something told him that this storm had caught her unaware. She didn't watch television and rarely listened to the radio. He knew that. The blizzard warning had come late too. Had she prepared for it? Was she all right?

This was the first blizzard of the season. That wasn't too bad for Minnesota. He remembered years when the snow started coming in October. Maybe it signaled an easy winter.

He couldn't shake this worry about Abbey. He opened the curtain once again and looked out. The storm wasn't breaking, and it didn't seem to have reached its full fury yet.

He checked the clock. Six a.m. Abbey was probably asleep.

God, could You please watch over her?

He felt better after asking for God's protection, but he remembered something from his childhood. A burden shared in prayer was halved. That's what his mother used to tell him. Any load was lightened by prayer, she'd explained, but that didn't let you off the hook. You still had to do what you could. It was a partnership.

Now he had to figure out what he should do. Blizzards limited his alternatives to, well, zero. But he'd figure something out. He had to.

The announcer's voice continued with his broadcast, which arrived in intermittent sputters.

Abbey peered outside. The storm whirled on, pausing occasionally, then increasing its intensity. She couldn't tell if it was growing worse or not.

She shivered—and only partially from the cold. There was something elementally terrifying about a blizzard, although she'd lived through enough of them to know that the safest place for her to be was inside. The problems happened when someone went outside and got stuck in the snow, or perhaps got turned around and lost.

It had happened to her once. She had been in college, walking home from the part-time job she had at a restaurant. She'd lived only a few blocks away, but the windborne snow was so intense that she'd had to walk with her head down and somehow had turned mistakenly. She'd ended up in an unfamiliar alley and had wandered for over half an hour before stumbling upon her apartment. She'd managed to escape frostbite, although her face had been swollen for a day from the icy blast of the snow.

This forced seclusion was going to drive her crazy. She cooked herself another cup of coffee, but it tasted terrible. She walked through her house, picking up the newspapers from the past week that had piled up. Then she straightened the towels in the bathroom.

What she really wanted to do was go to the store. The weekly sales figures were due, and there was the box of sweaters that had arrived late the day before. If they weren't unpacked soon, they'd be irretrievably wrinkled.

Of course, the power was probably off at the mall, so the computers were down, and the steamer would be useless, but she could do some of the work by hand, and if she took the sweaters out of the box and laid them out on the workroom table…

There was a break in the wind, and she could see her driveway. The area behind her car was blown clear, and an idea began to form in her mind. She could back out.

"No travel is advised…snow gates on the interstate

are closed…extremely slippery…finger drifts…" The radio crackled back into life.

The snow gates were huge metal gates that blocked the ramps to the interstate during a snowstorm, but they wouldn't affect her. She didn't use the interstate to get to the mall. And slippery? She'd go slowly. As for finger drifts, the long, narrow heaps of snow that stretched across a lane or two of traffic, they were no problem. She'd accelerate through them.

And besides, she reasoned, she'd stay just long enough to do the weekly report and take the sweaters out of the box.

She got dressed as quickly as she could, pulling on several layers. The temperature in her house was dropping, and according to the thermostat, it was already four degrees colder inside than it had been when she got up.

A blast of icy wind threw snow in her face as she opened the front door, and instinctively she tucked her head down as she scurried to her car. The man on the radio had been right. It was very slick, and she had trouble keeping her balance with the force of the wind.

She hurried around the back of her car and stopped. What she hadn't been able to see from the kitchen window was a huge drift that wrapped around the driver's side of the car, just out of her view. It was almost as high as the side mirror. It would take her forever to shovel it out, especially with this wind. She gave up and crept back inside, abandoning her plan.

The house, although there was a definite chilly edge to the air, was much warmer than outside. She kicked off her snowy boots and dropped her coat unceremoniously on the entryway floor. She was stuck here, and she might as well make the best of it.

Abbey wrapped herself in the throw from the couch and curled up. Maybe she could just sleep through it.

At first sleep seemed impossible, but the pound of the blizzard eventually lured her eyes to close and her breathing to even out.

Then the blizzard began pounding harder.

She sat up, groggily, and realized that the sound was coming from outside. Someone was knocking at her front door.

Chapter 13

Who could be at her door during a full-fledged blizzard?

Abbey paused for only a moment. On one hand, her visitor could be an ax-murderer, but on the other hand, this was a blizzard and no one should be out in it, not even an ax-murderer.

She peeked through the window in her kitchen. Another vehicle was parked beside hers. The snow was swirling so thickly that she couldn't tell what color the car was, just that it looked to be something with four-wheel-drive. Ax-murderers didn't drive four-wheel-drive vehicles, she was pretty sure of that.

She opened the front door a crack and saw a rather tall, huddled shape. It certainly didn't look like an ax-murderer.

He looked like Mike. A very cold Mike.

She threw open her door. "Come in!"

He stepped inside her entryway, and an eddy of snowflakes accompanied him. "Do you need firewood?" he asked without preamble.

"It's good to see you too, and yes, I do," she answered. Her heart was ridiculously elated to see him.

"Wait a second, then."

He vanished back into the storm and went to his car. Within moments he was back, carrying an armload of firewood.

She took it from him. As he kicked off his boots and shed his coat and muffler, she arranged the logs in the fireplace and started the kindling.

"I'm impressed." He spoke behind her.

"Why?"

"It's not easy to lay a fire and have it start that quickly. At least I've never been able to do it. I have a fireplace in my apartment, but I go through a lot of matches getting it started, and even then it doesn't always work out right."

Abbey rocked back on her heels. "It'll take a couple of minutes to catch. The trick is where to put the kindling, and to remember to put the logs in bark side down. My dad taught me how to do it. We used to camp out a lot."

"Really? You don't strike me as a camping kind of gal."

"I'm not. I never was. My parents were, though, so I got dragged along. I never did figure out the charm of cooking over a campfire. I always ended up with everything charred on the outside and raw on the inside. Plus sleeping in the woods is an open invitation to any biting, creeping thing to come along and bite and creep on you. What's the point?"

Mike stood behind her, rubbing his hands together, and she realized he must be frozen.

"Where are my manners?" she asked. "I have a visitor, and I haven't even offered him something to wrap up in."

He chuckled. "I wonder if Emily Post dealt with blizzard etiquette."

She gave him the throw from the couch. "Here, use this. I'm plenty warm here by the fire...er, the single little flame that will soon catch."

As if on cue, one of the smaller logs sparked into life. Abbey smiled. "Good. Now it's only a matter of time before the other logs catch too, and we'll have a real rip-roaring fire."

Mike draped the woven throw around his shoulders. "Great. That wind is fierce."

Abbey looked out the window. "Is it really bad?" An idea was formulating in her mind. If he could get to her house, then he could take her to the mall. It wasn't that much further.

"The roads are awful. It took me forever to get here. I had to go five to ten miles an hour the whole time."

"But you got here," she pointed out, smiling brightly.

"I hope you're not thinking what I think you're thinking," he said, "because the answer is No."

"How do you know what I'm thinking?" she asked somewhat peevishly.

"Let me guess. You'd like a lift to the mall."

"Okay, you do know what I'm thinking. Please,

Mike. I have so much to do." She felt like a child wheedling for a toy instead of an adult asking to be taken to work.

"No. The streets are dreadful." His voice was adamant, and he sat down squarely on the couch.

"But you got here," she repeated.

"And it was stupid, but I was worried about you."

"Which was stupid, driving here, or worrying about me?" The words were out before she thought about them.

His lips curved in a slow smile. "In this world, worrying about other people is not stupid, at least in my experience—well, I need to clarify. Maybe we're mixing up worrying and caring. Worrying is out of control, whereas caring is in control. When I start to worry, I know I need to take it to God. It's an alert to me that I'm not handling something well, but I know that God can."

She sat on the sofa beside him. "Only you would see worry as a call to prayer. The rest of the world worries about worry. Just check the cover of any magazine. 'Fifteen Ways to Worry Less.' 'Worried about What's Worrying You?' And I'm sure it's just a matter of time before someone comes up with 'Worry Your Way to a Slimmer, Trimmer You!'"

"Worry is a signal," Mike said, wrapping the blanket around him tightly. "Whenever you worry about someone, it's because you have a concern for them, usually for their welfare. Worry by itself is futile, but if you turn it into action and prayer, then it becomes helpful."

"I don't know about that," she said slowly. "I worry

about a lot of things, like the store, for example. I was even worried about Claire when I saw the blizzard."

"You're sweet to think of her. They do have an emergency generator out there, by the way, so they're nice and warm at Golden Meadows."

Abbey felt her muscles relax. She'd been more apprehensive about the elderly woman's situation than she'd allowed herself to recognize.

"No, worry isn't good at all. It consumes you and does nothing for the person you're worrying about," Mike continued, as if knowing where her thoughts had led her. "What we do when we feel worried is up to us. If there's something we can do to ease our concern, then of course we should do it."

"That's the hardest part," she confessed. "What if we can't do anything—like today, when the storm prevented me from getting out."

"That's when prayer comes in. We give it back to God, tell Him that we recognize our anxiety, and we trust Him. That's the sticky part—letting God do His work, having faith that He is at work, even when it isn't readily apparent to us. The problem is when we don't handle our concern well and let it take over our minds. That's worry."

The radio, which had been silent for some time, suddenly sputtered with static. "Situation improving…northern Minnesota…back to regularly…"

Abbey and Mike looked at each other and laughed. "Well," said Mike, "thanks for the update, huh? Sort of sums it all up."

She rose from the couch and looked out the window. "I think they may have been a bit optimistic about the storm. It looks as bad as ever."

She hugged her arms as she sat back down. "I don't know if I ever thanked you for bringing the firewood—I was so glad to see it…and you."

His warm brown eyes twinkled with a soft reflection of the fireplace's cheerful blaze. "My pleasure. See, this blizzard's not all that bad. You've got a fire burning; you've got a friend with you. What more could you ask for?"

"A cup of coffee."

He stood up and went back to the front door. She could hear him pulling on his boots and coat. Was he leaving? She stood up and joined him in the entryway.

"Was it something I said? Look, I can live without the coffee if that's what the problem is, although I personally don't see…" Her voice trailed off as she realized that under the muffler and pulled-up coat collar, he was smiling.

"I'll be right back."

"It's not that important—" she began, but he brushed away her concerns.

He vanished from the warmth of her house and was soon lost in the swirl of white. But within seconds he was back, and he held out a large blue vacuum bottle. "I made this before I left the house. The power did flicker back on for awhile early this morning, and I made a pot just in case. I can't believe I forgot to bring it inside with me."

Within minutes, they were both seated again in the living room, cups of coffee in their hands. As the fire warmed their faces, she felt her tension ease.

"This is the life," she said, a bit surprised at how relaxed she felt. Her usual reaction to being housebound would have been restless energy, and she had to admit, if she had been here alone, by now she would have been a nervous wreck. "I suppose I could get used to it, but I'd really have to try."

"You should. God didn't mean for us to spend our lives at work."

She studied him covertly. He talked so easily about God. His life must center around his faith. It was something she couldn't quite understand.

"Everything with you is God, isn't it?" she asked.

He had his head back and his eyes closed, and for a minute he didn't answer. She couldn't tell if he was sleeping or praying or just resting his eyes.

At last he opened his eyes and looked at her with his clear amber gaze. "Yes, it pretty much is. He is my life. Make that a capital L: Life."

"How did you come to that?" she pressed, finding that she really did want to know. "I mean, was it always like that, or did you have some kind of experience, or what? And please tell me if I'm being too snoopy."

"I'm always glad to share my story. I was raised Christian. I went to Sunday school and to church. I'd accepted Jesus as in I accepted Him without thinking, the same way you accept a bit of snow in the winter or a pleasant day in June. But when I really accepted Him in my heart and my mind and my soul was in church one Sunday. Are you sure you want to hear this?"

Abbey nodded. "Please."

"I must have been growingly aware of the lack of something in my life, but I couldn't put my finger on it. And then, one day in church, the gospel reading was the story of Jesus and the lame man. You know, where Jesus says, essentially, throw away your cane, your crutch, your mat, and get up and walk."

"That did it?"

"I realized at that moment that it was very simple. I had to put aside the 'canes' I used in my everyday life—for me, that meant the whole slew of excuses I'd use to get out of anything that would require me to lay my heart on the line, like I didn't have the time, or it was someone else's turn to do the work—and get up and walk on my own, with Him."

"And that's what you did."

"That's what I'm doing," he corrected. "It's all a process, which is why so many people refer to it as a path. I'm still walking and stumbling."

"I can't believe that little Bible story did all that," Abbey said. "I'd always thought it would be a big knock-you-off-your-feet experience."

"I was sitting down when it happened, so I can't speak to that," he answered, his eyes gleaming. "But even the little things are what make the big things happen. Like the fire. You started by lighting the kindling, little bits of wood that burn out quickly. But the kindling sparked the twigs, which lit the small sticks, which lit the logs."

"The Parable of the Fireplace."

He laughed. "Well, you get the idea. We now have a wonderful fire keeping us warm, and that's my point. From that one thin match came this great blaze."

"I don't know," Abbey said doubtfully. "I need to think about it."

"I'll pray for you," he said. "I can do it right now if you'd like."

The radio chose that moment to burst forth with renewed life and issue an updated weather bulletin: "…Storm has diminished…plows are out now… tomorrow…"

The lights flickered on, and the furnace clicked into operation.

"You don't need to," she said. "I think my prayers have just been answered."

Mike concentrated as he drove along. He knew he shouldn't be out yet, but with his vehicle in four-wheel drive, he'd be all right. And Golden Meadows wasn't that far away.

He'd had to leave. He knew now that more than anything he wanted Abbey to know the Lord the way he did. *That's asking a lot, isn't it?* he questioned God. He knew what the answer was.

She'd have to do it on her own terms, in her own way. For everybody it was different. He could feel her hunger for faith, her thirst for salvation. All he could do was give her the kindling and hope the fire caught.

His vehicle still hadn't warmed up, and at the first stoplight he rubbed his hands together. Now that the storm was over, the sun was out, making the late morning seem warmer than it was. Once the snow-plows got out and did their job, the only evidence of the morning's blizzard would be the deep piles of snow scooped aside by the plow blades.

God had asked him to watch over Abbey, and it was a burden he had accepted. Was what he had shared this morning too much—or not enough?

His advice to Abbey about worry came back to him. He could continue to worry, turning his thoughts over and over in his mind in the futile hope that he'd see something new there, or he could do what he should do. He could examine the reason for his concern and give it back to the Lord in prayer.

But the questions in her eyes did something strange to his heart, and for once it was very hard to take his own advice.

Chapter 14

A small snowplow was already clearing the lot at Golden Meadows. Mike pulled into a parking space and gave the snowplow driver a jaunty wave before dashing into the retirement home.

The snow had drifted against the west side of the doorway, and over the top of the pile he could just make out the curious faces of some residents who were checking the aftermath of the storm.

When he came through the door, they surrounded him, chattering about the excitement of the blizzard. One woman pushed her walker closer. "Wasn't that something, Sweet? We couldn't see past the edge of the parking lot!"

The fellow standing beside her frowned. "Snow is snow, Marlys. Don't tell me you haven't seen snow before."

The woman beamed at him happily. "Actually, I've never seen a blizzard before at all! I came here from Florida."

The grumpy man seemed somewhat abashed. "Well, a blizzard is just snow with some oomph, that's all."

Another woman, who stood behind him, rolled her eyes expressively. "It was exciting. They had to use the generator since the power went off. Did it go off where you were?"

Mike nodded. "But it's back on now."

He'd been scanning the group, but he hadn't seen his grandmother, which was unusual since something this exciting should have sent her down to watch the storm and its aftermath. Maybe she had gone to visit someone or to pick up an item at the small store here at Golden Meadows.

He asked about her, and the group discussed her absence with enthusiasm and concern. "I didn't see her at breakfast," the first woman said, "but a lot of people chose to stay in their rooms this morning. Storms do that to some folks. They just hole up."

"We had oatmeal with raisins for breakfast," the grouchy man offered. "There's some as what don't like that. Maybe that's it. I didn't come down because I can't abide raisins. Nasty little things. Stick in your teeth. Not a fan of oatmeal either. Horrid glop that tastes like somebody forgot to finish cooking it."

"Oh, John, you are such an old crank. Can't you lighten up?" Marlys said.

The man who had talked to Abbey and Mike about relationships joined the group. His long-sleeved shirt was neatly pressed, and he leaned on his cane. "Is Mrs. Thorson under the weather?"

"I hope not," Mike said, but he didn't like the sinking feeling in his stomach. Claire adored breakfast, especially oatmeal with raisins. If anything happened to her... It was too painful to even think about.

"I'm sure she's okay," Mike told them reassuringly, "but I'd better go up and see her."

"You do that," the man said, turning to leave. "She's a good woman, almost as good as my Eleanor, may she rest in peace. Tell her Albert Caldwell asked about her."

The group resumed their watch of the man on the snowplow as he continued to scrape the snow out of the parking lot.

Abbey attacked the snowdrift that locked her car in. She really needed to get a better shovel than the one she'd inherited with the house. This one was ungainly, and as much snow slid back onto its original spot as was left on the blade of the shovel.

She probably should have insisted that Mike take her along to Golden Meadows. Then she could have easily asked him to give her a ride to Cedar Mall.

Her back protested as a sudden realization brought her upright. She had never picked up the present from Aunt Luellen.

This was getting ridiculous. How hard would it be to go out there and pick it up? She made a mental note to go out there and get the gift later in the day, once the snowplows had cleared the roads...and she'd gotten out of her driveway.

She jammed the shovel into the snow and looked

at her handiwork. All she'd succeeded in doing was demolishing the drift from a smooth pile of snow into a ragged heap. But it was not a bit smaller.

Maybe if she backed out as quickly as she could, she'd clear it. It was worth a try.

She headed back inside to get dressed for work. There might even be enough hot water by now for her to take a shower.

The red light on her answering machine was blinking. She pushed the button and heard the voice of the manager of Cedar Mall, clearly reading a prepared message: "The lots are being cleared by snowplows, but to ensure the safety of the drivers as well as our employees, we are requesting that you do not come into work until the parking areas are done. The mall will reopen at five p.m. today."

She was tempted to ignore the dictum. Those reports were waiting, and she could get so much done before the mall opened. But she knew that mall management was serious when they made these policies, and she did not want to tangle with them. So she resigned herself to spending the rest of the day inside. There was a book on the end table that she had started reading in the summer that she could start in on again.

Abbey got the book and sat down with it. She opened it to the spot that was bookmarked and read for a few lines. It made no sense. She'd have to start it again.

Well, that was okay, she told herself. She could do that. She turned to the front of the book and began to read.

Coffee. Another cup of coffee would be nice. She

made a pot and sat down once more with the book. Two pages later she was up again, looking for something to eat.

"Oh, give it up, Abbey," she scolded herself out loud. "You're more antsy than an August picnic." She paced through the house until she finally sank down onto the couch.

It wasn't just the forced house arrest that bothered her. It was Mike...and what he'd said.

What exactly was it about him? She'd known him, somewhat, for many years, but lately their lives had become conjoined, primarily because of those goofy frog slippers that Aunt Luellen had sent to her instead of Claire.

Abbey had long ago taken the idea of loving someone and shelved it in the back of her mind, right next to religion. She had always intended that one day, when she was settled in her career, her MBA in hand, she would look into love and faith. But with Mike, they came perilously close to arriving hand in hand.

This wasn't the way she had planned it, not at all. She had plans for her life, a career plan. It was what she had talked to the young women at his church about.

What made her life work for her, what gave her days shape and meaning, was her career. She was good at what she did. She'd brought Trends back from being on the brink of closing to one of the most financially stable businesses in the mall. She had done it because she was focused. She'd started young, identified her strengths, and built on them.

What was wrong with that?

Aunt Luellen used to talk about the parable of the

talents. It was everyone's responsibility, Aunt Luellen had told her, to make the most of the gifts God had given them. Wasn't that exactly what Abbey was doing? And rather than running ahead, helter-skelter into the future, she'd laid out a path to follow.

The problem was that people kept stepping onto her path. People like Mike. And what had become painfully clear to her since her growing friendship with Mike was what she hadn't included in her plan: fun.

That Bible verse that was tucked into the toe of one of the slippers sprang to her mind: "This is the day which the Lord hath made; we will rejoice and be glad in it." That was Mike. He certainly was having a good time with God. Was that his secret?

The phone rang, and she leaped to answer it. It was probably mall management, telling her that the parking lots were cleared, so she could go to work... assuming she'd be able to back out.

But it wasn't the monotone voice of the mall manager. It was Mike, and he began without preamble: "Claire is ill. Very ill."

Chapter 15

Abbey paused in midmotion, the scarf she was knotting around her neck hanging from her numb fingers. She must have heard him wrong. "Ill? What do you mean? How ill?"

"She's feeling dizzy, and she says she has pains." Mike's voice was calm, but Abbey could hear the worry behind the words.

"What kind of pains? Chest pains?"

"No, stomach pains. Probably something she ate."

Abbey realized that the scarf was now trailing in her coffee cup, and she pulled it out and swabbed at it as she spoke. "Is she in the hospital?"

Mike hesitated a moment before answering. "She refuses to go."

"Refuses to go?" Abbey realized she was nearly

shouting and forced herself to moderate her speech. "Why on earth won't she go?"

Mike's pause was even longer, and when he spoke, Abbey could hear his stark fear. "She says she wants to die at home in her own bed."

Abbey's world collapsed. "Die?"

He spoke so softly she had to struggle to hear him. "She always said that when she died, she wanted to do it in her own bed, and preferably around Christmas. She wants to spend Christmas in heaven...where there's bound to be a birthday party the likes of which earth has never seen."

"No, no. She's not going to die, is she? She's not going to die! Please tell me she isn't." This was not the way things were supposed to happen. Abbey had just gotten attached to Claire. She couldn't let her go.

He became reassuring. "It's probably not that major—at least that's the sense I got from the nursing staff. A doctor did come in and check on her. Praise God that he had been on ER duty at the hospital and had walked over to visit his own father at Golden Meadows. It's just a short trip, but I guess it took him quite awhile since he waded through snow. The plows hadn't been out yet."

"Well, if a doctor has seen her..."

"But I have to be realistic."

"I don't like realistic." She was aware that she sounded like a little child, but that was exactly how she felt—small and powerless. Realistic was sickness and pain and parting. It wasn't good, especially now.

"She's not young. Every illness is a stress for her. All we can do is pray for her." The words hung in the air. "Please pray for her, Abbey." Then he hung up the phone.

Pray for her!

Didn't you have to be a Christian to do that? She didn't know how to pray, not really. She'd learned as a child that it wasn't right to pray for a bicycle—her aunt had straightened her out on that one—but that was about the extent of her knowledge on the subject.

She didn't want Claire to be sick, and she particularly didn't want her to die. *Please, please, make her all right.*

Well, she'd just have to leave the praying to Mike.

Abbey poured herself another cup of coffee and carried it into the living room. She sank onto the couch and didn't even bother with the pretense of trying to read one of the magazines piled on the end table.

Make her better.

She couldn't abide sitting here a minute longer. She had to do something. Abbey put her cooling coffee on the kitchen counter and pulled on her boots. She was going to go to Golden Meadows.

The sky was a bright, clear blue now that the storm had passed, and the sun hurt her eyes. The world looked sculpted in snow. *A single storm can change everything,* she mused. *One storm blows through and another takes its place,* she thought. *First snow, and now this. Her emotions were battered.*

The demolished snowdrift was still behind her car, and she studied it briefly. At just the right angle, she could make it through.

But then she saw the impediment that she could not cross.

The snowplows had been by, and the end of her driveway was blocked with the snow the plows had pushed in. Heavy chunks of compacted snow and ice lay in a thick, impenetrable ridge. There was absolutely no way to get through that with her car. It had to be shoveled out, or preferably taken out with a plow or a strong snowblower. All she had was this insufficient shovel.

Once again, she was ill-prepared for the storm. Abbey sighed. Was everything a metaphor?

She mounded her hands over the end of the shovel and rested her chin on her knuckles as she surveyed her predicament. She was really locked in now. It would take her all afternoon to break through…if she were lucky. Experience had told her that she was not getting out any time soon.

Thwarted by a snowstorm.

Hot tears pressed against her eyelids. Why did she even care about this old woman? And what did she hope to accomplish by going to Golden Meadows, anyway? It wasn't as if she could help Claire. She was a store manager, not a miracle worker.

Why did Claire have to get sick? And why couldn't she just go to the hospital? That's what most people did. They got sick, and they went to the hospital to get better. Why wouldn't she do it? This wasn't fair!

Abbey slammed her fist onto the side of her car. It was all wrong. Claire needed to be well.

She abandoned the effort to dig herself out and put the inadequate little shovel back into its spot in her garage and went back inside. She poured herself a fresh cup of coffee, but it was bitter on her tongue.

The coffee at Golden Meadows was good. She remembered the conversation with the man who had spoken to them on her first visit. His Eleanor was lucky indeed. Would Abbey ever find a love as real as theirs?

God, save Claire.

She paced through her small house. All she could think of was a single phrase: *God, save Claire. God, save Claire. God, save Claire.*

Suddenly her feet stopped their mindless steps. She was praying. She, Abbey Jensen, was praying! For the first time in years, she was praying for someone else. And it felt terrific.

She continued: *God, save Claire.* The words were simple, but they said it all. In her mind, she could picture the elderly woman, her nearly sightless eyes still alert behind the substantial lenses. The Bible, such a sign of her faith, centered in her room—as it must have centered in her life.

And those slippers. Those goofy frog slippers with the fake gemstone eyes. Claire hadn't even opened them yet.

What had Aunt Luellen written on the note? "Wishing you great hoppy-ness always." That's what Abbey wanted for her too. Great hoppy-ness.

"Don't spend Christmas with God," she whispered to Claire. "Spend it with me."

Mike held the gnarled hand and gazed into his grandmother's eyes, which opened and closed irregularly. "Grandma, go to the hospital."

Claire shook her head. "I'm staying here. I'm around the people I know. Sweet, for us here at Golden Meadows, death isn't quite the scary ogre it is for you young folks. It's not wearing a big black cape and reeking of the grave. It's simply how we get from this life to the next. Kind of like a bus."

He laughed. "Only you, Grandma, would come up with that. Death is like a bus. But this bus isn't yours. Yours is waaaaaay across town."

She patted his arm. "When my bus comes, Honey, I'm hopping on. Destination: Promised Land!"

"Plus it's almost Christmas," he reminded her. "You know how much you love Christmas. You wouldn't want to miss that, now would you?"

"Christmas! That reminds me. Help me sit up, Sweet."

"Oh, Grandma, do you think you should—"

"Hush your mouth and help me. I'd hope by now you'd know enough to listen to your elders. I'm not going to run a marathon. I just want to sit up." Her china-blue eyes twinkled weakly.

He gently lifted her thin shoulders and helped her edge up to a sitting position. "Good?"

"Super. Now, you have to get Abbey out here. I've got her present, you see. She never did pick it up." Claire leaned forward and whispered conspiratorially, "She's a bit absentminded, I'm afraid."

Mike smiled at that. "I suspect she likes coming out here to see you more than she lets on, and that present is just an excuse."

"Do you think so?" Claire seemed very pleased.

"By the way, a gentleman named Albert Caldwell asked me to relay his concern."

His grandmother sat up straighter and patted her puff of white hair. "He did? Did he say anything else?"

"We—"

A knock at the door interrupted them. It was the doctor who had checked on Claire earlier.

"Sweet, do you mind for just one minute?" Claire asked. "I'd like to talk to Dr. James for a moment alone."

Mike hesitated, but the doctor nodded and said, "Go ahead and wait in the lobby. I'll stop by before I leave and give you an update."

"Then you can come back up and see me. But if you can find me a piece of chocolate, that'd be nice," Claire said. Then, as if suddenly tired, she sighed. It was the sigh that worried Mike. His grandmother wasn't a sigher.

He did the only thing he knew to do: he prayed. *God, make her all right. If she needs to go, I'll try to understand. But I love her, and I want her with me a little while longer. I need her.*

This prayer came with a postscript that totally surprised him: *And Abbey needs her too.*

Dr. James joined him in the lobby and, after updating the other residents on Claire's condition, invited Mike into the Fireside Lounge. Most of the chairs were filled, and their arrival created a curious stir, but the two men managed to find a fairly secluded spot.

"I'll tell you what I know," the doctor began, "which is that I don't know. She seems to be as healthy as a horse, although, of course, the horse is eighty-two years old. She seems to have good moments and bad moments, but her mind is sharp."

"That's true," Mike agreed. "What concerns me is

that she seems to be willing to let go so easily. She's not fighting any of it."

"In most patients, that would be a worry," the doctor said, "but with Claire, I see it more as a natural acceptance. She's certainly not hurrying toward death."

"Not racing to catch her bus," Mike murmured.

"Excuse me?" Dr. James was clearly confused.

"Just vintage Claire," Mike said.

Abbey's pacing had slowed down, simply because her legs were getting tired. She hadn't heard anything more from either the mall or from Mike. How could all her worries come together like this on one single day…and just before Christmas too?

She stared at the phone, her arms clutched across her chest. If only she could will the phone to ring!

As if by telepathy, it did just that.

She lifted the receiver, dreading the mall manager's drone. But instead it was Mike.

"The doctor checked on her again, and they're going to keep her here at Golden Meadows tonight. If her condition worsens, they'll move her to the hospital pretty much whether she wants them to or not. The hospital is less than a block away, and for now she's comfortable in her own room. They can monitor her there for the time being."

Abbey breathed a grateful sigh. "It sounds like she's going to be fine."

"I'm still being cautious. She can still use our prayers."

She paused. "I prayed for her."

There was a long silence. Abbey wished she could see his face to know how he was reacting. Then he said, simply, "Thank you. By the way, she wants to see you. She still has your present."

"Oh, I forgot! I'm getting as loopy as Aunt Luellen. But I'm not going to be able to get out until I get ahold of someone to plow me out. The snow fairies didn't come in and dig out my car or my driveway."

Mike promised to come by the next day and either get her car out or give her a ride to Golden Meadows, then to work.

"Tomorrow's Christmas Eve," he reminded her.

Chapter 16

Abbey awoke to the sound of a snowplow outside her window. She leaped off the couch where she'd fallen asleep and stumbled to the front door. She opened it a crack. Mike was out there, a blade attached to the front of his four-wheel drive vehicle. He waved at her, and she wiggled her fingers back at him before retreating into the bathroom to pull herself together.

One look in the mirror confirmed her worst suspicions. She looked horrible. One side of her face was wrinkled where she'd slept on it, and her eyes were puffy and swollen. She hoped that Mike wouldn't hurry with his plowing outside. Maybe he'd go slowly and give her the necessary time to make herself presentable. Nobody, she reasoned as she splashed water on her face, deserved to see her looking the way she did when she first woke up. It was enough to scare a bear back into hibernation.

One side of her hair bent straight up, and no amount of combing would make it settle down. In desperation, she clipped a barrette in it. It didn't look very good, but this was no time for vanity. She wanted to get to Golden Meadows and see how Claire was doing.

She'd caught only a glimpse of Mike's face, but it had been enough to know that the news from the retirement home must have been good. Plus, he wouldn't have stopped to plow out her driveway if his grandmother was still gravely ill.

She had just pulled on a red sweater when he knocked on the door.

"Thank you so much," she said as she let him in. "How's Claire?"

He smiled. "Much better but still weak. She's holding her own, and I think we'll have her around to tell us how to live our lives for quite awhile."

Our lives. The words had a glorious ring to them.

"Are you ready to go?" Mike was wrapping his muffler around his neck.

She gulped down a final splash of coffee. "Ready."

It was odd, she thought as she rode to Golden Meadows with him, how much everything about her had changed. Just a month ago she would have done anything to avoid going to the retirement home. Now she couldn't wait to get out there.

And Mike. He had changed her in ways she wasn't yet ready to explore. What was especially strange, she mused, was that she was still changing, and it was a wonderful sensation, like a butterfly must feel when it finally emerges from its long cocooned sleep.

Perhaps she was just caught up in a generally good mood. It was the day after a storm, the sun was shining, it was Christmas Eve morning, and Claire was doing better.

Mike's car was already warm, and Abbey's lack of sleep began to catch up with her on the drive to Golden Meadows.

He glanced over and grinned as she yawned. "Big night?"

"I couldn't sleep, worrying about Claire, so I decided to watch *It's a Wonderful Life*. I just bought it the other day, and I still hadn't seen it all the way through."

"So what did you think?"

"A bit predictable."

"Really?" His eyebrows arched in surprise.

"But sometimes predictable is good, very good." Her smile threatened to wobble out of control as she added, "Last night I would have taken predictable."

"No kidding. I was so scared about Grandma. I must have talked God's ear off. I couldn't stop praying." He pulled into the parking lot of the retirement home. "Well, here we are."

He turned off the car engine and sat, his hands still on the steering wheel. "Can you give me a minute here? I need to get a little strength before I go in."

Abbey reached over and touched his arm. "Please, pray aloud."

"Dearest Father, thank You for another morning, for a blessed morning, as we approach Your Son's birth. Abbey and I ask that You keep Grandma in

Your healing hands. We love this woman." He paused. "Amen."

"I'm not very good at praying out loud," he confessed as he helped Abbey out of the vehicle. "I know what I'm saying in my heart, but when I say the words out loud, it sometimes seems too little."

"I'm sure God listens to both your heart and your lips," Abbey said.

Mike's quick smile told her how much he appreciated her comment.

They were mobbed as soon as they opened the front door of Golden Meadows.

"How's she doing, Sweet?"

"Tell her I've been praying!"

"She'll pull through. She's a strong one."

"A good Christian woman."

"That Norwegian blood, it's going to keep her going, that's for sure."

Mike laughed as their voices assailed him. "I'm going to go up and see her, and I'll tell her you're all thinking of her and praying for her."

Claire's eyes were shut when they entered her room, but they flew open as if spring-loaded. "Sweet! Abbey!"

"Merry Christmas, Grandma," Mike said, dropping a kiss on her forehead. "How are you feeling?"

"Better. A little on the woozy side, so I'm afraid I'll have to pass on the ice-skating. Remember, Sweet, how we used to go ice-skating on Christmas Eve? The moonlight on the pond made it look like we were skating on a huge diamond."

Mike laughed. "I'd almost forgotten about that! We'd pretend that the diamond belonged to us, and we'd decide what we were going to buy with the money we'd get when we sold it."

Claire turned her bright blue eyes toward Abbey. "What would you buy?"

"Skating lessons, to start with. I'm afraid I'm probably the only Minnesotan who's a total klutz on the ice."

The elderly woman beamed happily at her. "When I met Arthur, I could have skated circles around any Olympic ice-skater, but I pretended I didn't know how, just so I could hold his hand. Silly fool, he fell for it. He couldn't skate for beans, but I sure did like to hold his hand."

A beeper sounded. Both women looked at Mike, who had the grace to be abashed about the interruption. "Sorry. I got this pager, but I never thought anybody would ever page me on it. Grandma, can I borrow your phone? It's the store."

After a quick conversation, he hung up the phone and turned to them. "I've got to run. The cash register won't start up. Abbey... ?"

"Oh, no." Claire looked as disappointed as a child who'd just lost out on candy. "I wanted to watch Abbey open her present from Luellen."

Abbey looked at Claire, at the forlorn expression on her face, and made a decision: "I'll stay. I can take a cab back."

Claire beamed happily. "Good."

Mike hugged his grandmother and promised to be back later. Then he left them alone together.

"Abbey, Dear, I know you need to get to work, especially with this being Christmas Eve and all, so I won't keep you long. It's just that I'm so anxious to find out what Luellen gave you." Claire wiggled with barely subdued enthusiasm.

At that moment, a health-care aide knocked on the door and entered, pushing a metal cart covered with a white linen napkin. "Claire, I have some breakfast for you. It's your favorite—French toast. I knew you had guests, so I brought some extra."

Claire's eyes lit up at the sight of the French toast, but she glanced at the Christmas present. She was clearly torn between finding out what was in the package from Aunt Luellen and having the French toast, so Abbey resolved the issue for her. "I'd be glad to join you for breakfast. We can open the package when we've eaten."

Abbey was amazed at how hungry she was, and she mentioned it to Claire, apologizing for gulping down her meal.

"Young people don't eat enough anyway," Claire said. "Everybody worries about being thin, although I don't know why. What's the point of dieting all the time? Especially when you can't have chocolate. I love chocolate."

Abbey smiled. Claire was really a dear.

"I know you have to get back to your store, Abbey, but I really do want to see what Luellen sent you. She always sends such interesting gifts." Claire motioned toward the tiny tree. "It's over there. Could you get it for me, please?"

The package was wrapped in gaudy green foil sprinkled with golden stars. "I wonder if this paper came from Brazil."

"Chile, Dear. Luellen's in Chile. Open it so I can see what it is!"

Abbey pulled the paper off the box. Inside was an elegant leather-bound pocket calendar. "It's beautiful!" she exclaimed as she examined the burgundy, tooled leather. "Look, Claire, there's even a spot for one of those teeny electronic gizmo things that does everything but park your car!"

As she handed it to Claire, a piece of paper fell out. "Of course! It just wouldn't be a gift from Aunt Luellen without a note."

"What does it say?" Claire asked expectantly.

"Wow. This is short for Aunt Luellen. It just says, 'As you plan your days ahead,' and then 'This is the day which the Lord hath made; we will rejoice and be glad in it.'"

"Ah." Claire nodded her head as if that explained it all. "From the Psalms."

"That's the same one that was in—" Abbey said, stopping before she could spoil the surprise of Claire's slippers, which remained unopened under the Christmas tree. "But why—" And before she could finish the question, she answered it.

Because Claire, whose days were limited, looked forward, while she, who had her whole life ahead of her, planned only by an hourly schedule at work. The Lord, the one that Mike spoke of so easily, existed for her too, and He gave her each day as fresh and new and bright as each day that He gave to Claire.

The same God made them all. The same God. This was why Mike and Claire were so happy—they were rejoicing in each day that the Lord had given them. It didn't matter if she had a thousand days...or one. They were all gifts.

The iron bars that had held her heart imprisoned

fell away. She was free, totally free now to love…
and to be loved. An aura of happiness and well-being
surrounded her, too new and fragile to be analyzed
or explained. She knew what she had to do. She had
to tell Mike.

"Can I borrow your phone, Claire?"

Just exactly what she was going to say to him, she
had no idea. She just knew she wanted him to be with
her right now, to be at her side as she explored this
wonderful sense of freedom.

But Mike wasn't at his store. The employee who
answered the phone said that after Mike unjammed
the cash register, he had run over to the church to
drop off some toys he was donating for the Christmas
Eve service. So Abbey kissed Claire goodbye with a
promise to come back later and fairly flew down the
hall to the lobby.

Too bad she didn't have her car with her. She
could have zipped right over there, but instead she
was forced to wait for a taxi.

And wait she did. She watched the clock over the
door of the lobby as the minutes slowly ticked by.
Selma assured her, when Abbey called every five
minutes, that the store was doing fine. Both Selma
and Brianna were on duty and wouldn't need Abbey
there until noon.

Nadine, the desk clerk, emerged from the office
with a young woman at her side. "Miss Jensen!" the
teenager exclaimed.

Her face was familiar, but it took Abbey a minute
to realize where she'd seen her before.

"I'm with the Jeremiah Group. Remember, you

came out and talked to us?" She stuck out her hand awkwardly and said, "I'm Mona, by the way."

"Mona, it's good to see you again," Abbey said. "Do you work here?"

"I do now," the young woman declared. "Something you said got to me, and I had a talk with the career counselor with the Jeremiah Group, and bingo. Here I am. I want to be a nurse, I think."

"That's great! Nursing is a wonderful, noble career."

"I have you to thank for it too," Mona added shyly, her eyes darting down to study her shoes.

Warmth surrounded Abbey's heart. "That's so sweet," she said. "Thank you for saying that. You know, I wasn't too sure that anything I said that evening had an impact at all."

"It wasn't anything you said. It was what you wore."

"Excuse me?" Abbey couldn't believe what she was hearing.

"Oh, not that it was gross or anything. It just made me realize that I didn't want a job where I had to dress up everyday like that. So when I thought about what I did want to wear, I always saw myself in a nurse's uniform. I figured, hey, nobody's going to come to my door and hand me one. So I decided to go out and get it myself. And this is where I'm starting. I've even signed up at the university to start on my degree."

Abbey was overwhelmed. She remembered Mike's words: "Who knows, you may very well have touched someone's heart here today in a way you can't know." And in turn, today, that someone had touched her heart.

"Mona, good luck on your new career. I know you'll be an outstanding nurse." She couldn't resist adding, "And you'll look smashing in a nurse's uniform."

Mona left with Nadine, and Abbey was left alone to wait for the cab. What a day this had been! Truly it was one to rejoice in!

While she waited, she prayed and rejoiced and turned her newfound knowledge over and over in her mind. At last the cab arrived, and Abbey decided to have the driver take her directly to the Word of Faith Community Church to save time.

The small church looked like Christmas itself, with glistening white snow drifted around the brick walls. The steeple sparkled in the morning sunlight, and the cross at the top of the spire pointed straight to heaven.

Mike was arranging gift-wrapped packages around a small tree in the narthex. He smiled when he saw Abbey. "How does it look?" he asked, stepping back to look at his handiwork.

"A pile of Christmas presents could never look bad," she said.

"You've definitely been with Grandma," he said. "Her Christmas spirit has been rubbing off on you! What happened to your humbug disposition, Scrooge?"

"It's gone. There's…something else there instead."

"Wow, that's a change. Cool!"

"That's not the only thing that's changed," she said, suddenly shy.

He stopped and stared at her, a gaily-wrapped package dangling from his fingers, forgotten for the moment. "What do you mean?"

"I mean I'm different. I mean that all the pieces fell into place. They've been there, bit by bit, but this morning it all came together. This is the day that the Lord has made, you know? Every day is the day. Every day is, all by itself, the most tremendous gift we have." She rubbed her forehead. "Am I making any sense?"

"Oh, yes," he said softly. "You're making a lot of sense."

"Good, because I want to talk about it, but I don't know exactly what to say. This Christianity thing needs some kind of manual."

"It has one. It's called the Bible."

"I don't know why I'm telling you this."

"I think I do," he said softly. "At least I hope I do."

He took her hand and looked into her eyes. "I have prayed for this moment for a long time, almost hoped against hope that this would be the one prayer that God would grant. And He has blessed me beyond belief. This is my Christmas gift from Him, knowing that you are His."

For a moment, neither of them spoke, until Mike broke the silence. "Would you like to go into the sanctuary with me?"

She nodded, and he guided her into the darkened sanctuary, with only the light from the stained-glass windows to illuminate it. "I love that this room is called the sanctuary. I think of all it means—a haven, a safe place, a refuge—and I know that I'm in His presence."

They stood together, absorbing the atmosphere. "When I'm here," Mike continued, "the rest of the world falls into the background. I can focus on Him.

It's a special place, beyond explanation. God is very real to me, Abbey, very real. I can't imagine trying to live without Him—or wanting to."

There, with the scent of the Christmas tree in the narthex, the wreaths by the coat racks, and the candles on the altar, Abbey thought of the little Baby who was born so long ago and yet had been born again two thousand years later in her own heart. She thought of His death and resurrection and knew, in that moment, that He lived in her heart. She gave her life to God, and her heart sang the wonders of the first birth long ago…and of the birth that had just happened in her.

Mike watched her face as she was transformed. He had prayed for this. He knew that this was God's plan, and he was but a part of the plan.

I don't ask for much, God, he began, then almost laughed. That wasn't true. He'd already asked for Claire's recovery only slightly more than an hour ago. *Okay, I usually don't ask for much,* he revised his prayer. *But if I could have one more thing. Just one more…*

He paused before proceeding. Was he asking too much? Would God reject his plea outright?

Abbey looked at him, her eyes glowing, and he knew he had to continue.

Please, God, let her love me.

Chapter 17

Abbey stared at Mike. Could it be true? Was what she was seeing in his eyes real—or was it just a mirror of her own?

Without the prison walls around her heart, she could see so much more. Had she always loved him, or had it just happened? As she put out her hand, she realized it didn't matter. Either way, she loved him.

The words were extraordinarily simple. She loved him. And, possibly, just possibly, he loved her too.

She felt absolutely liberated by the thought.

"Excuse me." A voice echoed in the empty sanctuary from behind them. "Mike, the store just called. The cash register is jammed up again."

The magic hovered around them a moment longer, until they both smiled.

"Tell them I'm on my way," Mike called back.

Then his glance returned to Abbey, and so did the magic. "Can you come to the Christmas Eve service with me tonight?"

"I'd be delighted to." And she meant it.

Christmas was full of presents.

The day flew by. Selma and Brianna barely had time to tease their boss about her new attitude. Abbey sang with the mall's Christmas carols. She bought a cinnamon-flavored sucker at Lollipop Time, and by the time lunch rolled around, it was already gone. She got polka-dotted socks with individual toes in them for Selma. She stopped at Piñata Pete's and purchased a piñata shaped like a cow for Brianna.

It was Christmas!

But at last the mall closed. The recalcitrant metal grating slid down to close Trends.

"Whew!" Selma said. "I think we managed twice the sales that we did last year. At least that's what my aching dogs are telling me." She leaned over and massaged her swollen feet.

"We did do better. I haven't run the sales record yet, but—"

"What?" Selma said, in mock horror. "You, Miss Retail-Is-My-Life, you can't quote me our receipts? You're slipping, Gal!"

Brianna pushed her coworker toward the door. "Leave her alone, Selma. Can't you tell our boss is in love?"

"You two!" Abbey protested, but she couldn't dispute it. They were right.

"There's something else going on," Selma said

thoughtfully. "Something else has made Abbey different. Softer."

"Love will do that," Brianna told her.

"Well, sure, but this is something else. What's up, Boss Lady?"

Abbey reached for her purse. "It's very simple. A Baby born in a stable touched me. A star over a small town on the other side of the world touched me. A flock of angels singing in the heavens touched me. Christmas touched me."

Selma and Brianna stopped. Then, they looked at each other and smiled. "All right!" Brianna said, hugging her.

"Hallelujah!" Selma echoed. "That's wonderful news!"

"It is," Abbey agreed. "It is."

"We'd better get going," Selma pointed out, "or we'll still be here when people start rolling in with returns on the twenty-sixth. Eight a.m., right, Boss?"

Abbey groaned. "Unfortunately."

The two women picked up their packages and purses and prepared to leave by the delivery door in the back of the store.

"See you two the day after tomorrow," Abbey said. "Have a very Merry Christmas!"

"And a Merry Christmas to you too!" Selma called. Brianna waved a cheery farewell.

Abbey hurried down to Tuck's Toys. She walked through the gamut of the deserted kiosks, most of which would be gone after the returns and sales had ended in a week or two. She'd miss them when the mall went back to its normal schedule and appearance.

Unless, of course, the mall management decided to go with a King of Hearts theme or something equally as bizarre for Valentine's Day. She could see it now; Kiss Me Kandies next to Love in Bloom Florists.

But somehow it wasn't as dreadful as it had first seemed. Maybe falling in love had softened her.

She paused at the now-abandoned Candy Cane Calaboose and remembered the time she and Mike were locked in there together. Well, she mused, even the Candy Cane Calaboose wasn't bad if you could fall in love with your cellmate.

A horrible realization struck her. She didn't have a present for Mike.

On the wall, a poster for the Candy Cane Calaboose fluttered by a single staple. An idea struck her, but she'd have to hurry. She tore down the poster and ran back to Trends. One of the last shipments had been picture frames, and she held her breath as she looked through the display, searching for one in particular.

She breathed a sigh of relief. It was there.

The frame itself was a series of interlocking candy canes, and the poster fit perfectly inside it. She wound some tissue paper around it and stuck it into one of their gift bags. She dug through the remaining stock of complimentary small gift cards until she found one with a candy cane on it.

Abbey chewed on the end of her pen. She couldn't think of a thing to say on a card. "You're very sweet" was very dumb. "I CANEn't live without you"? "We were MINT for each other"?

It was always difficult to be clever. Sometimes it

was downright impossible, and this was one of those moments.

She opted for no card at all. After all, she'd be handing him the gift in person.

Her eyes scanned the shop for a gift for Claire. Then she remembered something that had come in that morning's delivery. She had opened the box, but she had gotten so busy that she hadn't had the chance to unpack it and put the contents out. She dashed into the storage room and dug in the box until she found it.

It was a blue-and-white china jewelry box. The blue exactly matched Claire's eyes. Impulsively she tucked a gaily-striped candy cane pin inside it.

She tied it up in bright red paper, then wrote a sales receipt for the items so she could pay for them the day after Christmas.

"Ready to go?"

Abbey jumped as Mike's voice echoed throughout the cavernous mall. "You startled me!"

She shoved the hastily wrapped packages into a bag. "I'm going out the side. I don't trust this rusty old gate to work right tonight, and I sure don't want to be late."

He handed her a take-out bag as she met him in the mall corridor. "Not too fancy—just a burger and fries from Boomtown Burger. I've got two cans of soda in my coat pocket too. We'll have to eat on the run, or I'm afraid we'll be late."

The church service was wonderful, Abbey thought. The carols had a meaning far beyond what they had portrayed while they'd played on an endless loop at the mall, and she sang along with heartfelt gusto.

At the end of the service, ushers passed out small candles with circular cardboard drip-stoppers. The lamps dimmed, and the minister began: "I am the light of the world..." One by one the church members lit their candles from their neighbor's as the light was passed from the minister to the last guest, until the entire sanctuary was lit only by the glow of a hundred candles. And one by one they blew out their candles after the benediction while singing "Silent Night."

Abbey could not bear to speak until they had left the church and were standing outside, the cold air turning their breaths into clouds. A light snow had fallen, making everything freshly white.

Her heart had opened honestly, and she needed to face life—all of it—honestly. She turned to Mike, her emotions overflowing, and started to speak, but he put his finger over her lips.

"Sssh," he said. "Listen."

From inside the emptying church, the faintest sounds of the last notes of "Silent Night" drifted out. "It's the Christmas prayer, the search for silence," he whispered.

She held his hand until the last notes faded away. "Thank you for giving me this Christmas Eve," she told him. "There's something else I wanted to tell you."

She had to open up, she simply had to, or she would burst with the joy of it. "Mike, I—"

He bent toward her, and time stood completely still. They were the only ones in the world. They were everyone. Then, he kissed her.

It was true. She heard bells. Big loud bells that played "Joy to the World."

He laughed as their mouths separated. "Perfect timing," he said, motioning toward the spire where the bells rang out the Christmas carol.

If it were possible to save time, to press it between the pages of the calendar so that she could take it out and look at it again and again, this would be the moment she would save, Abbey thought. It was perfect, completely and totally perfect.

"Abbey, I think I'm falling in love with you." His words carried across the wintry night, and two of the people leaving the church heard and bent their own heads together.

There was so much she wanted to say, but the words stuck in her heart. Instead, she stood on her tiptoes and kissed him gently, reverently, in answer.

"I'd love to stay here and kiss you in the moonlight," he said at last, "but there's another woman in my life, and I've promised her I'd go out to Golden Meadows to play Christmas carols for a sing-along. Want to come?"

But Claire didn't join them in the Fireside Lounge. She was asleep, the aide told them. It was a calm, healing sleep, though, not the fretful tossing and turning that had signaled her illness initially.

The sing-along was attended by a majority of the residents, many with holiday sweaters and ties on. It was the perfect way to end the perfect Christmas Eve, like a bow on the present of life.

The next morning, Mike picked Abbey up early. "Grandma's waiting, anxiously I'm sure, to open her presents. She likes to dig in before breakfast, but I've told her she'd have to wait a bit later today."

"She's like a kid about Christmas, isn't she?" Abbey asked. "It's wonderful to see that enthusiasm."

Claire was sitting up, looking much better than she had, when they arrived. "I've got the presents ready," she announced. "Let's go!"

At her insistence, Mike helped her out of the bed and into the overstuffed blue chair. Abbey suppressed a grin at the yellow frog slippers that she slid her feet into. Clearly Claire hadn't waited for her and Mike before starting to open gifts.

With a flurry of paper and ribbons flying, Claire unwrapped her presents. She oohed over the Wag-A-Muffin and the sweater that Mike gave her and aahed when she opened the jewelry box from Abbey.

"This has been a wonderful Christmas," Claire said. "And these are terrific presents. Thank you both."

"The best Christmas gift of all," Abbey said, giving Claire's hand a squeeze, "is seeing you healthy again." Then she looked at Mike. "Slight correction. It's one of the best presents."

"What? What?" Claire asked, her eyes glowing with excitement.

"This may be a bit premature, Grandma, since I haven't checked it out with Abbey, but I think there might be a wedding in the future." He dropped a kiss on Claire's forehead. "That is, of course, if we have your blessing."

Claire wriggled even straighter. "I have a problem with this, Michael James Tucker."

"You do?" Mike's face flushed. "Grandma—"

"I can't believe that you didn't ask her first!" Claire

scolded. "Now, get down on your knees and do it properly."

"Yes, Ma'am!"

Mike gave her a jaunty salute and dropped to one knee. Taking Abbey's hand in his, he said, "Abbey, we've known each other since we were kids. We've been through many changes, some good, some bad, that have taken us apart from each other—and brought us back together again."

His voice caught in his throat, and he had to stop and take a deep breath to keep his words even. "I want to spend the rest of our lives together."

Abbey could only hold on to his hand as if it meant life itself. Her lips opened and closed, but no sound came out. Perhaps it didn't need to.

"Abbey?" His forehead wrinkled in concern. "Are you all right?"

"Yes," she said, her voice somewhere between tears and laughter. "Yes, yes, yes!"

"Kiss her," Claire commanded from her chair. "That's the next step. Sweet, do I have to think of everything?"

Mike playfully shushed his grandmother. "I know what I'm doing."

Claire gave a good-natured snort. "Ha. Well, it's a good thing I'm here in case you mess something up. Go ahead."

"Thanks," Mike said, grinning at her. Then he fished in his coat pocket and pulled out a box that was about the size of a small popcorn bag. "Okay, let me explain. See, when you've got two lovely women in your life, what are you going to do on Christmas?

Clearly, get them the same thing. Abbey, here's your Wag-A-Muffin."

She opened the box and pulled out a pure white dove, embossed with a golden cross on the wing, a golden collar around its neck. "It's beautiful!" she said, running her hand down its back and watching the dove's tail move.

"I'm glad you like it. But now here's my dilemma. I got Grandma a sweater, and it just didn't seem right to get you one too."

"It's improper," Claire interjected. "The first gift you give someone shouldn't be clothing."

"See what I put up with?" Mike said teasingly. "But then I realized that these old rules are for the birds, so I went ahead and got you something to wear."

Then he continued to stand there, his hands in his pockets, smiling at her.

"Where is it?" Claire asked impatiently. "I want to see!"

He didn't say anything for a moment, until at last he said, "Abbey has it already."

"I do?" she asked in surprise. "What?"

"Look closer at the dove. It's got a collar on…"

Abbey gasped as she realized what the collar was. It was a simple gold band set with a single clear diamond.

"If you don't like it, we can go pick out another one."

"I love it," Abbey managed to gasp, once her heart had returned to beating in a fairly normal pattern. "It's beautiful!"

He slipped it on her finger, and for a moment they

stood together, their gazes locked in a timeless embrace. "Now do I kiss her?" he asked over his shoulder to his grandmother.

"Now would be a good time," Claire said, and before her eyes shut, Abbey caught a glimpse of Claire's satisfied smile.

"I have a present for you too," Abbey said at last. She handed her gift to Mike. "I was going to wait, but now I think this is the right time."

Mike opened the framed picture and grinned. "I love it!" Then his eyes met hers. "Does this mean what I think it does?"

"I think I knew that you were my destiny when we were locked up together in that silly Candy Cane Calaboose. I thought I'd hate it, but deep inside me, I wanted it to go on and on." Abbey gave him a tremulous smile. "Isn't that funny? When I was locked up with you, I found my freedom."

Her heart was no longer imprisoned in its cage of defiance. She was free now, in so many ways. The walls were down; the door was unlocked and open, ready to welcome love.

"Grandma," Mike said at last, "you need to get healthy and stay that way. I think we have a wedding in our future!"

Claire wiggled her toes happily, and Abbey was sure she saw the frogs on the yellow fuzzy slippers smiling.

Epilogue

The Word of Faith Community Church was packed. A gentle snow had fallen, but it did nothing to diminish the happiness of those gathered within. It was December twenty-fifth, and this was a wedding. There was little that people liked more than a Christmas wedding.

It had been a year since Abbey had accepted Mike's proposal, and the days since then had flown by as if winged. The only change was that as the days passed, she loved him more.

The blessings in her life had grown and intensified since that amazing Christmas Eve. God continued to touch her life daily. She saw it in her work as well as her love. God did care for His own.

She'd gone back to college, preparing for the MBA she'd always wanted. Mike had come home one day with a brochure about distance education classes, and she'd signed up right away. They were perfect for her schedule.

After a period of relatively ineffective resistance, she'd answered the call to work with the Jeremiah Group. Her focus area was appearance, and she now advised the young women on the proper clothing to wear to work and how to find appropriate yet inexpensive apparel.

Mona had easily established herself as one of Abbey's favorites. Her natural affinity for the elderly served her well at Golden Meadows. Mona had even started college with a nursing degree as her goal, and Abbey was as proud as a mother peacock. As matter of fact, the young woman was presiding over the cake table at the wedding reception.

"Your veil's crooked." Selma's voice caught, and although Abbey saw the glimmer of tears in her friend's eyes, she knew they were tears of happiness.

"I can't go in with my veil crooked," Abbey teased her gently. "People will talk."

Selma sniffed back the threatening sobs. "They will anyway."

"Honey?" Her mother's hand caressed Abbey's cheek. "The usher says it's time to seat me, so I have to go. Abbey, I love you. Mike will be a good husband, I can tell."

"Any last words of motherly advice?" Abbey asked shakily.

"Just love him. That's it. Just love him."

Her mother started to go, then turned back. "I think I need to modify that a bit. Love him simply. Don't get carried away overanalyzing him. But also don't forget that you are a child of God too. Be careful not to lose yourself." She paused. "I didn't know that when I first got married—or maybe I did, and I just ignored it—but it kept both Ed and me from having the best relationship we could, and that wasn't fair to any of us, including you."

Abbey saw tears pool in her mother's eyes. "Mom, I understand. And it's all right. Even when I was a teenager and fighting back against anything and everything, I still knew, in my heart, that there was love in our house."

"And one more thing, Abbey. Always, always trust God. Again, your dad and I didn't have that trust, and it made marriage just that much harder. But now we know, and life is better. I'm so happy to know you're starting your married life with God as the head of your household."

"Oh, Mom." It was all that Abbey could manage.

Her mother laughed shakily. "Look at me. The wedding hasn't even started, and already I'm a sodden mess. I need a handkerchief."

"So do I," Abbey confessed, feeling her emotions starting to crescendo. "We'd better get this show on the road," she told her mother. "If I start crying now, I'll have a drippy nose and swollen, red eyes by the time I get to the altar. Mike will turn and run."

Her mother smiled mistily, gave her a quick kiss, and left to be seated in the sanctuary.

"Ready?" Brianna spoke to them from the door of the room where Selma and Abbey had dressed. "We've got a church full of people anxious to see you. Some of them are worried about getting back to Golden Meadows in time for the Christmas party there, so I think you'd better get moving before they mutiny."

"All right. I'm ready. Nervous as a cat, but I'm ready." An entire flock of butterflies seemed to have made their home in her stomach.

Selma smoothed her red velvet bridesmaid's dress. "Next time, I get to be the bride, okay?"

"Okay. You've got to find your own fellow, though."

Selma made a face. "I knew there was going to be a catch somewhere."

Abbey enveloped Selma in one last hug. "I'm so happy," she confided. "I think I could burst."

"Well, don't," Selma said practically. "That's a new dress you've got on, you know, and white stains like nobody's business."

Abbey left the room with Selma and joined the rest of the bridal party in the small area behind the sanctuary, which was decorated in red and white. She adjusted her bouquet, which, like those of the others in the bridal party, included tiny candy canes sprinkled among the red and white carnations.

She leaned down and kissed her matron of honor, whose wheelchair was festooned with garlands of red and white tinsel.

The music started, and the four women proceeded down the aisle.

I should remember this, Abbey thought as she passed through the wedding guests. Their faces blurred, but she knew they were all smiling at her. *I need to remember this always.*

The minister was waiting for her at the altar...and

so was Mike. He had never looked so tall, so capable, so trusting.

The minister began to speak the familiar words: "Dearly beloved, we are gathered…"

Her mind wandered back to the day the socks dropped through the grating, to the time of the blizzard, to the afternoon in the Candy Cane Calaboose.

"I do."

She looked at Mike, and the world got smaller, the congregation vanished, and there was only the two of them.

"I now pronounce you husband and wife. You may kiss the bride."

The world exploded with joy. The minister turned them to face the congregation. "I'd like to introduce to you Mr. and Mrs. Michael Tucker."

The organ burst into glorious song, a collection of Christmas carols, and hand in hand, Mike and Abbey rushed back down the aisle and into the narthex.

"We're married, Honey," he said to her as he took her in his arms. "Now and forever."

He bent to kiss her, and as she lifted her lips to meet his, the guests began to file out.

Claire was the first to get to them. Abbey leaned down to hug her, and the older woman beamed at her. "Weddings are so romantic, aren't they?" she cooed. She blinked her eyelashes flirtatiously at her companion. "Albert, do we have something to tell them?"

The gentleman whom Abbey had met in the coffee shop during her first visit to Golden Meadows looked fondly at Claire. "Would that be advising them to keep Valentine's Day open?"

"What are you two planning?" Abbey asked. "A party?"

Albert and Claire's eyes sparkled with a shared secret. "Perhaps," Albert said.

"You could call it a party," Claire said, "except that we prefer to call it a wedding."

Abbey reached for both of them and enveloped them simultaneously in a bear hug. "I'm so glad for you!" She knew she was gushing, but she couldn't stop.

"And don't think you can just recycle the gifts from this shindig that you don't want," Claire said with an impish grin. "I'll be watching."

Abbey turned to Mike. "Did you know anything about this?"

He shook his head. "Nope. I'm as surprised—and as pleased—as you are. Grandma kept this locked tighter than the closet where she used to hide our Christmas presents."

"Well," Claire explained, "I had to get you two together first."

Mike grinned. "I don't know what to say, except thanks and congratulations!"

"By the way," Claire continued, "I do have another surprise. Want a hint?"

"Sure!" Abbey said.

"Okay, here it is: Great hoppy-ness always." The elderly woman motioned toward the entry to the church.

Abbey turned startled eyes to the door. "Aunt Lu-ellen! You came all the way from Brazil?"

"Chile, honey, and of course I did. I couldn't miss seeing my favorite niece get married!" The woman was tanned and fit and didn't look half of her eighty-something years. "And I can't wait for you to see what I got you!"

"If it turns out to be half as good as what you got me last Christmas," Abbey said, "I'm going to love it!"

Aunt Luellen looked confused. "I can't remember what I got you last year."

Abbey looked up at her handsome new husband. "Love," she said. "That's what you gave me."

* * * * *

REQUEST YOUR FREE BOOKS!

2 FREE CHRISTIAN NOVELS
PLUS 2
FREE
MYSTERY GIFTS

HEARTSONG
PRESENTS

REQUEST YOUR FREE BOOKS!

2 FREE INSPIRATIONAL NOVELS
PLUS 2
FREE
MYSTERY GIFTS

Love Inspired

REQUEST YOUR FREE BOOKS!

2 FREE INSPIRATIONAL NOVELS
PLUS 2
FREE
MYSTERY GIFTS

Love Inspired
HISTORICAL
INSPIRATIONAL HISTORICAL ROMANCE

YES! Please send me 2 FREE Love Inspired® Historical novels and my 2 FREE mystery gifts (gifts are worth about $10). After receiving them, if I don't wish to receive any more books, I can return the shipping statement marked "cancel." If I don't cancel, I will receive 4 brand-new novels every month and be billed just $4.74 per book in the U.S. or $5.24 per book in Canada. That's a savings of at least 21% off the cover price. It's quite a bargain! Shipping and handling is just 50¢ per book in the U.S. and 75¢ per book in Canada.* I understand that accepting the 2 free books and gifts places me under no obligation to buy anything. I can always return a shipment and cancel at any time. Even if I never buy another book, the two free books and gifts are mine to keep forever.

102/302 IDN F5CY

Name	(PLEASE PRINT)	
Address		Apt. #
City	State/Prov.	Zip/Postal Code

Signature (if under 18, a parent or guardian must sign)

Mail to the Harlequin® Reader Service:
IN U.S.A.: P.O. Box 1867, Buffalo, NY 14240-1867
IN CANADA: P.O. Box 609, Fort Erie, Ontario L2A 5X3

Want to try two free books from another series?
Call 1-800-873-8635 or visit www.ReaderService.com.

* Terms and prices subject to change without notice. Prices do not include applicable taxes. Sales tax applicable in N.Y. Canadian residents will be charged applicable taxes. Offer not valid in Quebec. This offer is limited to one order per household. Not valid for current subscribers to Love Inspired Historical books. All orders subject to credit approval. Credit or debit balances in a customer's account(s) may be offset by any other outstanding balance owed by or to the customer. Please allow 4 to 6 weeks for delivery. Offer available while quantities last.

Your Privacy—The Harlequin® Reader Service is committed to protecting your privacy. Our Privacy Policy is available online at www.ReaderService.com or upon request from the Harlequin Reader Service.

We make a portion of our mailing list available to reputable third parties that offer products we believe may interest you. If you prefer that we not exchange your name with third parties, or if you wish to clarify or modify your communication preferences, please visit us at www.ReaderService.com/consumerchoice or write to us at Harlequin Reader Service Preference Service, P.O. Box 9062, Buffalo, NY 14269. Include your complete name and address.

LIHDIR13R

Reader Service.com

Manage your account online!

- Review your order history
- Manage your payments
- Update your address

---

*We've designed
the Harlequin® Reader Service
website just for you.*

Enjoy all the features!

- Reader excerpts from any series
- Respond to mailings and special monthly offers
- Discover new series available to you
- Browse the Bonus Bucks catalog
- Share your feedback

Visit us at:

ReaderService.com